MELONHEAD
AND THE
WE-FIX-IT COMPANY

ALSO BY KATY KELLY

Melonhead

Melonhead and the Big Stink

Melonhead and the Undercover Operation

Melonhead and the Vegalicious Disaster

Lucy Rose: Here's the Thing About Me

Lucy Rose: Big on Plans

Lucy Rose: Busy Like You Can't Believe

Lucy Rose: Working Myself to Pieces and Bits

MELONHEAD
AND THE
WE-FIX-IT COMPANY

BY KATY KELLY
ILLUSTRATED BY GILLIAN JOHNSON

A YEARLING BOOK

Text copyright © 2013 by Katy Kelly
Cover art and interior illustrations copyright © 2013 by Gillian Johnson

All rights reserved. Published in the United States by Yearling, an imprint of Random House Children's Books, a division of Random House LLC, a Penguin Random House Company, New York. Originally published in hardcover in the United States by Delacorte Press, an imprint of Random House Children's Books, New York, in 2013.

Yearling and the jumping horse design are registered trademarks of Random House LLC.

Visit us on the Web! randomhouse.com/kids

Educators and librarians, for a variety of teaching tools, visit us at RHTeachersLibrarians.com

The Library of Congress has cataloged the hardcover edition of this work as follows:
Kelly, Katy.
Melonhead and the We-Fix-It Company / by Katy Kelly ; illustrated by Gillian Johnson. — 1st ed.
p. cm.
Summary: In the Capitol Hill neighborhood of Washington, D.C., eleven-year-old Adam "Melonhead" Melon and his best friend Sam try to stay out of trouble for a whole month to earn a fabulous reward.
ISBN 978-0-385-74165-1 (hc) — ISBN 978-0-375-99016-8 (glb) — ISBN 978-0-375-98668-0 (ebook)
[1. Behavior–Fiction. 2. Washington (D.C.)–Fiction. 3. Humorous stories.] I. Johnson, Gillian, illustrator. II. Title.
PZ7.K29637Mj 2013
[Fic]–dc23
2012034038

ISBN 978-0-307-92970-9 (pbk.)

Printed in the United States of America

10 9 8 7 6 5 4 3 2 1

First Yearling Edition 2014

To the girl cousins,
Emily Bottorff, Marguerite Bottorff, and Sally Rizzoli,
who have always been each other's greatest cheerleaders,
confidantes, and safety nets. You were born lucky.

1

THE BEAST

I was going to call my invention Melonhead's Courage Detector.

My best friend, Sam Alswang, double nixed that idea. "The Beast is a better name because it sounds terrifying, which it is."

"Like Boy versus the Beast," I said. "Who will win?"

"More like Man versus the Beast," Sam said. "Because you have to be manly to try."

"True," I said. "Also Boy because you have to be a certain age to enjoy this contest. Luckily, we are."

So far, we've challenged the Beast six times. And so far, Sam and I have equal courage.

The Rules of the Beast

1. The Beast is always liquid.
2. One week you are the Beast Maker. The next week you are the Beast Drinker.
3. If it doesn't make you gag, it's not the Beast. It's just gross.
4. Every formula is different. Every Beast gets its own nickname.
5. The most ingredients the Beast can have is six. The least is two.
6. The Beast must be safe to swallow.
7. The Beast must be made of food.
8. Boogers are safe to swallow. They are not food.
9. The Beast is only served on Saturdays.
10. One serving equals two gulps.
11. When you're done, you have to slam down your cup and scream "The Beast!"
12. No complaining.
13. No do-overs.

My last Beast recipe was prune juice, pickle juice, one drop of Tabasco, a spoonful of caramel topping, and a pinch of pulverized peppermint Altoids. I named it the Gag-O-Matic. It was. Believe me. If you don't, ask Sam.

Last week Sam mixed grapefruit juice, soy sauce, anchovies, melted mint chocolate chip ice cream, and two drops of Tabasco. You don't have to use Tabasco, but we always do. Sam named his formula Last Month's Garbage. I said, "Good name, because that's exactly what it tasted like."

After my first swallow Sam told me anchovies are small fish.

"I don't know how anchovies look in the sea," he said. "But the ones that come in a can have bones that look like hair. You already swallowed some."

Knowing about the hairy bones made the second gulp worse than the first. I congratulated Sam for that.

This week's Beast was made by me. I call it the Destructionator.

2

BRAINFLASH OF BRILLIANCE

Sam yelled from the sidewalk. "What's up, gorilla butt?"

"I need a BOB," I told him.

BOB stands for Brainflash of Brilliance.

"About the Beast?" Sam said.

"The Beast is a major BOB," I said. "The Brainflash I need is how to get my mom to give me an allowance. She says not until I'm a better spender. Also she's afraid if I have money I'll buy trouble."

"Did she bring up the X-ray glasses?" Sam asked.

"That is exactly what she brought up," I said.

"I told her it doesn't matter how long you wear

them, you can't see through people's clothes," Sam said.

"Two months is a lot of trying," I said.

"Did you remind her that we learned from our mistake?" Sam asked. "She appreciates that."

"She said the mistake was telling all the fifth-grade girls that the X-specs worked. There were complaints."

"Mothers of girls are sensitive," Sam said.

"Incoming mini-BOB," I said.

A fact about BOBs: You can't control when you'll get one.

"What is it?" Sam asked.

"You ask your parents for an allowance. If they say yes, my parents might give in."

"Ask? I've begged," Sam said. "My dad doesn't believe in free money. Even worse, I must face the Destructionator."

I bowed like I was a butler from London, England. "Your bread is on the windowsill, Bill."

Before you Challenge the Beast, you have to eat a wad of bread. It puts a pillow in your stomach. Then the Beast has something to land on besides your guts.

Sam dusted ants off two slices of white bread, mashed the slices into one bread ball, and bit it like an apple.

"The Beast is waiting in the kitchen, My Duke."

"Lead the way, Jay."

"After you, Sue."

We cannot stop ourselves from rhyming.

On Capitol Hill, where we live, Sam and I are known for being rhymers. Lately our fame has been spreading all over Washington, D.C. Sam's cousin Ella told kids at Temple Mica about the hilarious rhyme that got Sam and me sent to the school counselor for a talk called Inappropriate Words. His name is Mr. Pitt. He is annoying times infinity.

I kicked the kitchen door open. I didn't mean for it to hit the wall so hard. Sometimes I'm shocked by my own strength.

"Where's your mom, Tom?" Sam asked.

"Out back, Jack. She's getting revenge on the slugs."

"Where's your dad, Comrade?" he asked.

"In Florida, helping Congressman Buddy Boyd get reelected," I said.

"Egg-zee-lent," Sam said like he was a vampire. "Zee Beast needs pry-vee-cee."

My mom can't know about the Beast. It's for her own protection. She is a huge worrier with a giant imagination. Her main worry is Dangerous Things That Could Happen to My Son, Melonhead. Only she calls me Adam or Darling Boy. I'm trying to break her Darling Boy habit. Step One is switching to DB.

Not telling is also for my protection. If my mom knew about the Beast she would call Dr. Stroud to see if drinking disgusting things is normal behavior for eleven-year-old boys. My mom does not think courage needs to be tested.

My dad understands the ways of boys. But if he knew about the Beast, he'd tell my mom out of loyalty. In one shake of a rattlesnake the Beast would be out of control, because my parents are in a pact with Sam's parents. Whenever we get in a situation, they tell each other. Even though most of the situations are unpredictable and a shock to Sam and me, we get a consequence. Then, my dad and I have to discuss the Melon Family Guidelines for Life. His top Gs for L are *If in Doubt Ask an Adult* and *Why This Was Not a Freak Accident and Could Have Been Avoided* and *Think Before Doing.*

But from now on, situations and incidents, as my mom calls them, are in our past. The code name for our plan is OZ. That stands for Operation Zero. For the next thirty days we are following the G for Ls. We are thinking before we act. We have our reason. Her name is Aunt Traci.

3

THE BRIBE

Four days ago Aunt Traci brought my mom a book called *From Wild to Wonderful: Transform Your Child in Thirty Days!* My mom gave it back because: 1. It was one of Aunt Traci's books that caused the last incident; 2. My mom likes me the way I am; 3. I am not wild, I am spirited.

I was thinking *Yay, Mom!* until I found out that Transforming Your Child means bribing your child.

Only, the book calls bribes "rewards."

"I'll do it," I said.

Aunt Traci said, "Try it, Betty."

"No," my mom said in a firm way.

Aunt Traci acted like my mom said "Please sign him up this minute."

"Of course, it's no good making Adam wonderful if you don't put Sam on the program," Aunt Traci said.

My mom said that Sam is not her child.

"*Wild to Wonderful* inspires children and is a gift to parents," Aunt Traci said. "I can prove it."

Later, when we were out back helping Uncle Ben grill corn, Aunt Traci asked Sam and me if we wanted to be in a secret experiment.

I was about to say we're wild for experiments.

"We're spirited for experiments," I said.

"Some of ours are secret," Sam said.

"If you boys can go thirty days without getting into a situation, I'll reward you with a trip to Follies Amusement Park in Pennsylvania," Aunt Traci said. "Thinking about Follies Park will keep you on track."

"It will?" Sam asked.

"It's foolproof," Aunt Traci said. "And painless. You'll have fun. Your mom will see that I was right. Everybody wins."

"My mom's against *Wild to Wonderful*," I said.

"And Mr. Melon likes people to listen to his wife," Sam said.

"Honey, your mom and dad are going to be thrilled with the new, tamed you.

"And, Sam, your parents will thank me. Betty tells me your baby sister is quite a handful," Aunt Traci said.

"Only if a handful is a good thing," Sam said.

In case it wasn't, I said, "Julia's not even two and she's already hilarious."

"Handful means Julia's, um, energetic," Aunt Traci said. "My baby sister was a handful."

"Your baby sister's my mom," I said.

"She was wild before she was wonderful," Aunt Traci said.

I nearly lost my balance. "My mom was spirited?"

Aunt Traci laughed.

"OK," I said. "We'll take the bribe."

"Bribe?" Aunt Traci said. "My word. I'd never *bribe* anyone. When I do a good job at work I am *rewarded* with financial benefits. Why shouldn't kids get the same thing?"

"We're getting finances! Like allowance?" I double socked Sam's arms. "Hot diggity, ziggity dog!"

"Goodness, no," Aunt Traci said. "*Wild to Wonderful* says children don't understand money."

"Maybe newborn babies don't," I said. "If I didn't understand money, I wouldn't have spent the whole summer begging for an allowance."

"Ditto," Sam said. "I keep telling my parents, an eleven-year-old needs money."

"We know a measly nine-year-old who gets allowance," I said.

"Allowance is your parents' decision," she said. "I'd be overstepping if I gave you money."

Overstepping what, I don't know.

"Rewards, treats, and presents are all aunt territory," Aunt Traci said.

"Roller coasters are my kind of reward," I said.

"I have an idea," she said. "Since my friend Myrna gave me a pile of half-off admission coupons for the Follies, I think it would be okay to let you spend some of what we save on souvenirs. *Wild to Wonderful* doesn't have anything against coupon savings."

"What if my mom wants the old me back?" I asked.

"All she has to do is cut out the rewards and abracadabra, you'll be the same interesting and spirited boy that you are right now," Aunt Traci said.

"Can we go on the Fear Machine unlimited times?" Sam asked.

"It goes zero to sixty miles per hour in four seconds in the dark. The only things visible are horrors," I said. "There's an ax man, and your face gets brushed by spiderwebs."

"You may stay on the Fear Machine as long as your heart desires—all you have to do is stay out of situations for thirty days."

"No problem," I told her.

"That's thirty days in a row," Uncle Ben said.

"In a row?" Sam said.

"What if there's a freak accident and we get sucked into a situation?" I asked.

"If it's not your fault, it won't count," Aunt Traci said.

"If it is our fault, do we get a consequence?" Sam asked.

"No!" Aunt Traci said. "This book's philosophy is that children should never be punished. It's bad for their self-esteem. If you get into a situation you just won't get a reward."

Now that I have Follies Park on my brain, not getting the reward would feel like the biggest punishment anybody ever got.

"Don't you worry, Aunt Traci. Sam and I have stick-to-it-tive-ness."

"Remember, we're not telling your mom until the thirty days are up," she said. "Otherwise she won't be thrilled and surprised."

"If this works, our parents will see that we're mature enough for an allowance," I said.

This is Day Four of OZ. Zero situations. To be safe we're doing nothing except watching TV. Luckily, it's Shark Week. Unluckily, next week is not.

"Challenging the Beast is the first fun thing we've done since we started *Wild to Wonderful*," I told Sam.

"Head to the kitchen and pass the glass," he said.

4
BOTTOMS UP

Sam and I handwalked down the hall, through the dining room, and into the kitchen. We regular walked out the back door and looked over the porch railing.

"Hi, Mrs. Melon."

"Hi, Mom," I said.

She looked up. "Don't lean over so far, DB. It's a long drop."

"Who's winning the slug war?" I asked.

"The slugs," my mom said. "They ate their way through my lettuce last night. I'm setting traps."

"You're not killing them, are you?" Sam asked.

"Slugs make decent pets, Mom. Not as good as dogs, but they don't shed."

"We're not having pet slugs," my mom said.

"Okay," I said. "Enjoy staying outside."

"Bring on the Beast," Sam whispered.

When I'm the Beast Maker, I hide my concoction in the back of the fridge, behind my grandma's bread-and-butter pickles that nobody likes.

I handed the glass to Sam.

"Presenting Destructionator," I said.

He stuck his gum to the back of his hand and said, "It's day nine, Porcupine."

Sam's trying to win the world record for most days chewing the same gum.

"How does it taste?" I asked.

"Like the stretchy band on underwear," he said.

"Interesting," I said.

"Plus prickly," he said.

"From what?"

"Hair," he said. "Thanks to Bad Mad."

Sometimes our teacher Ms. Madison is Decent Mad. Twice she's been Good Mad. But we started off calling her Bad Ms. Mad. It stuck to her like Melonhead stuck to me.

Ms. Mad has Built-In Gum Sonar. If her BIGS goes off, it's goodbye, recess, hello, Reflecting Table. During school Sam sticks his gum wad behind his ear. Getting hairy is a side effect. We don't deduct classroom time from Sam's record.

Sam smelled the Destructionator. "No stink. No sludge. Looks like V8 juice. What's in this Beast?"

"No hints," I said. "I'm completely clueless."

"Julia could drink this," he said.

"You're wrong, King Kong," I said. "I wouldn't let your baby sister in the same room with Destructionator. Too dangerous."

"E-Z P-Z."

"Wait and see-zee," I said.

"Bottoms up," Sam said.

That's a real expression invented by adults. It has nothing to do with butts, though.

Sam snapped his head back, squinched his eyes, and dumped the Beast into his mouth.

His eyes popped.

His body shook.

He gurgled.

He gagged.

He turned into a human lawn sprinkler.

Luckily, the only things in the way of the spray were the sink, the chili pot, and me.

"Yow-wow-ow!" he screeched. "No fair using straight hot sauce!"

"One: I didn't. Two: It's hot sauce plus pizza sauce and cider vinegar. Three: It doesn't count if you upchuck."

Sam wiped his tongue on his Stoddard Soccer League T-shirt. It left a light red trail across the picture of the Capitol.

"The Beast is supposed to taste repulsive," he said. "But it's cheating to make it unswallowably hot, Melonhead!"

I felt like he could be right.

"Okay, you get credit," I said. "For courage."

"I'd better. My throat feels like a Slip 'N Slide covered with nose slime and killer bees," Sam said.

Then he sneezed.

I wiped my forehead on a dish towel. "It's mostly nose slime, I'd say."

Sam yanked open the fridge and chugged Low-Fat Vanilla Hazelnut Irish Dream Cream. It's supposed to make coffee taste decent.

"Be glad my mom's not watching," I said. "She calls drinking from the carton a germ multiplier. Ditto spit and flying mucus. Also schools, elevator buttons, trash cans, and doorknobs."

Sam didn't say anything.

I felt bad for criticizing my mom. "To be fair, most ladies are anti-mucus," I said. "Not just my mom. Bad Ms. Mad's motto is Sneeze in your elbow. Ditto Madam."

"How come nobody cares if you get snot on your elbow?" Sam asked.

Madam and Pop are our friend Lucy Rose's grandparents. Also Sam's and my best adult friends. They live four blocks from the Alswangs and five blocks from the United States Senate. We drop by for snacks two or three times a day. I mean Madam and Pop's, not the Senate. We only go there when we're bike riding down Capitol Hill and are too starving to pedal home.

You have to scrounge for Senate food. We have to wander the halls until we find a Reception sign. When we do, we stand semi-near adults so people

will think we're their kids. We help ourselves to sodas and mini-cheese blocks. True luck is when we get there after guests are gone and before cleanup. We help ourselves to all the leftovers. For payback, we bring our spare cheese to Madam and Pop. Plus curly tooth-picks for Lucy Rose. Most of them still look new.

By the way, it's not stealing. Reception food gets thrown away. We are preventing government waste.

"My tongue's still raging," Sam said.

"Squirt chocolate syrup on it," I said.

"Doesn't help."

He took the chili pot out of the sink and put his head in it. The sink. Not the pot.

"Turn the faucet to super cold," I said. "Now stick your tongue in the water."

That's when I saw the great discovery.

"You have power puke!" I screamed.

Sam stood up fast. His head hit the faucet and water flooded his hair.

"Look at the pot! Everywhere your throw-up landed, the copper is shining orange. Your amazing stomach acid eats dirt!"

"Find another acid maker," Sam said. "I'm retired."

"What if Benjamin Franklin said 'I don't feel like flying a kite in the rain and getting shocked by lightning'?"

"He must not have felt like it, because he didn't do it," Sam said. "Ben Franklin had the idea. Thomas-

François Dalibard did the lightning experiment. And he did it without a kite."

"Well, Thomas-François Dalibard did not refuse to help Ben Franklin," I said.

"I wouldn't refuse to help Ben Franklin," Sam said. "He didn't give me numb tongue."

"Bet you can't say 'numb tongue' three times fast," I said.

He said he couldn't because he had numb tongue, but numb or un-numb, it's impossible.

Sam looked out the window. "Red alert! Mom on the steps."

My mom is not the sort of lady who would enjoy having a two-tone pot. Especially if she knew it was caused by puke.

Luckily, Sam and I are the fastest of the fast. By the time she opened the door, the chili pot was in the hall closet, under a pile of rain boots.

"Ready for lunch?" she asked.

5

POP'S SICLES

Sam and I scarfed down our peanut butter and banana sandwiches.

"We'll eat the cherries on the walk to Popsicle Madness," I told my mom. "We like to plant the seeds on the way."

"Don't keep the footpool waiting," she said. "And remember to thank Pop."

A footpool is a carpool for people who can't drive.

The people in our pool are Pop's granddaughter, Lucy Rose; plus her top friend, Jonique; our sort-of-new friend, Pip; and Sam and me. Walking to school is fun if you're with a load of kids. Also, we have no choice because: 1. Washington, D.C., doesn't have school buses; and 2. We have the kind of parents who think kids should only get a ride if it's hailing. Hail is another thing we don't have in Washington, D.C. Well, we do, but hardly ever.

Pop always meets us at Congress Market so he can pay for the Madness. He says that's his way of thanking the company for naming Popsicles after him. That's a joke. Not the part about paying. That's real.

"If I ever get an allowance I'll take a turn buying," I told Pop.

Madam called me thoughtful.

Pop invented the Madness. He felt sorry that the only place the footpool ever went was school. Pop doesn't approve of some things that go on in schools. Like memorizing dates when we could be learning about black holes in space or the life cycle of a grub bug. He's also against all the sitting that happens in classrooms. I agree. When I oversit, I get energy buildup. That never turns out well.

Madam usually comes with Pop. Only she gets the fake Popsicles that have fruit clumps in them.

"If there's only one grape, I call it," Pip said.

"Cherry," Jonique said.

"Any flavor for me, but I'm the distributor," Lucy Rose said.

"Green or blue for me and Melonhead!" Sam said.

They go for flavor. We go for colors that make our tongues look sick.

The distributor is the person who gets everybody's Popsicles out of the freezer. When everybody gets their own, too much frost escapes. Then the owner says we're wasting his energy.

Lucy Rose likes to dig around the bottom in case there's a root beer flavor. That's only happened once.

After Pop paid, he and Madam sat on the bench in front of the store. The footpool sat wherever we wanted, which was mostly on the sidewalk.

"Have you written any songs today?" Pop asked Lucy Rose.

"One. It's about broken hearts and loneliness," she said. "It's for Deepali Sharma. She's my babysitter who got dumped by her boyfriend."

"You are a thoughtful friend," Madam said.

"Yes, I am," Lucy Rose said. "You can tell she's suffering, because she walked off before I finished verse five."

"Which is the best verse," Jonique said.

"What have you been up to, Pip?" Madam asked.

"I had to clean out the bread box," she said. "When I was throwing away the stale stuff I found a Moon Pie in the back. I put it in the microwave until it swelled up. Then I ate it."

"You do your chores on Saturday morning?" Sam asked.

"At my house you can't go out until they're done," she said.

"What have you two been doing instead of chores?" Madam asked Sam and me.

"Inventing supersonic vomit," I said.

"No kidding?" Pop said.

"Would I kid about vomit?" I asked.

"Yes," Pop said. "Frequently."

"But not when it's a scientific discovery," I said.

"You did not discover vomit, Melonhead," Lucy Rose said.

"Since when is puke an invention?" Pip asked.

We told about Sam upchucking the Destruction-ator and the pot spots. "His stomach acid literally ate the dirt off of metal," I said.

"Remarkable!" Madam said.

"Thank you," I said.

"Hold the plane!" Sam said. "I just realized! It can't be my stomach acid. The Destructionator made a U-turn at my tonsils. My acid stayed in my stomach."

"But how could it be so powerful without acid?" I asked.

"We have to go experiment," Sam said. "Thanks for the Sicles, Pop."

"Anybody want to come with us?" I asked.

"We can't," Jonique said. "We're going to work on our diorama about ancient Greece."

"We're making columns," Pip said.

"You would not believe how much toilet paper I had to unroll to get seven cardboard tubes," Lucy Rose said.

"What did you do with the toilet tissue?" Madam asked.

"I tore it in four square sections," she said. "I made stacks. It's more deluxe than on the roll."

"Let's roll," Pip said.

Not the toilet paper kind. "Let's roll" is Pip's double-meaning expression. It means let's roll like get going. Plus, let's roll like literally get rolling because of our skateboards and her wheelchair.

6

THE EXPERIMENT

Sam and I walked around my house hollering for my mom.

Then Sam noticed. "There's a note on the kitchen table, Mabel."

I could tell it was from my mother by the handwriting. Also because on the top it says A Note from Betty and has musical notes with faces.

I just got the joke.

> DB,
>
> I'm taking Mrs. Dubois to Eastern Market for groceries and to Baking Divas for coffee. If you're scared to be home by

*yourself, call me. Or you can go next door
and wait with Mr. Dubois. Or go to Sam's
house. But tell me before you go anywhere.*

Love,
Mom

*P.S. Don't use the microwave while I'm gone.
Or anything electric. Or sharp. Or hot.*

"Thank you, Mrs. Dubois, for not being able to drive anymore!" Sam said.

"She always gives us can't do's when we're starving," I said.

"We're always starving," Sam said. "How long does it take to go grocery shopping with Mrs. Dubois?"

"Long," I said. "She has bunions on her feet."

"I always thought those were called onions," Sam said.

"Time to work, Kirk," I said.

"First find food, Dude," Sam said. "My stomach feels like an empty paint can with a slosh of melted Popsicle."

I gave him the last handful of Trix cereal from my

cargo pocket. A lot of it was Trix dust. It's colorful but not filling.

"I'll hunt for food," I said. "You get the Destructionator ingredients."

Our fridge was stuffed with what my dad calls slim pickings.

"There's mayonnaise, cheese that's moldy on purpose, and a load of Dee-Lite-Full diet yogurt."

"I'm not allowed to eat fake sugar," Sam said.

I hit gold in the freezer. "Potato skins with sour cream, cheddar cheese, and bacon crumbs," I said.

"We can't use the microwave," Sam said.

"Skins are tasty at any temperature," I said. "By the time we finish Destructionating, they'll be thawed and perfect."

I got paper and a pen from the everything drawer. "You keep the log, Dog."

"We can't write a scientific log on A Note from Betty," Sam said. "It's unprofessional."

"We'll recopy it when we're famous," I said.

"We have to figure out if one ingredient is the powerful one or if it's a combination," Sam said.

"We test each thing by itself," I said. "Then two

ingredients mixed. Then we'll test the Destructionator."

"Each mixture gets a number. That way no mix-ups," Sam said. "Plain pizza sauce is number one. So you paint number one on the chili pot. Number two: hot sauce."

"Number three is vinegar," I said. "Write: Doesn't stick to pot."

"Test four: pizza sauce plus vinegar," Sam said.

Test five was pizza sauce plus hot sauce. Test six: hot sauce and vinegar. Test seven: Destructionator.

7

BOY GENIUSES

"Hot diggity double dog in a fog!" I said.

"Holy cannoli," Sam said. "Numbers one, four, five, and six are orange. Number seven is glowing! Destructionator wins!"

"Mega-BOB!" I yelled. "Remember what Mr. Santalices said about tomatoes?"

"They're a fruit, not a vegetable," Sam said. "Ditto for hot peppers. Ditto anything with seeds."

"Right!" I said. "And fruits have acid."

"That is a major Brainflash of Brilliance!" Sam said. "From the taste of it, I bet vinegar has acid too."

He was dead right.

I hooted my head off. Sam whooped. I did a vic-

tory jump over a kitchen chair and somersaulted into a handwalk across the kitchen tiles. Sam karate-kicked the air a lot and a chair once.

We sat on the counter and ate defrosted potato skins dipped in leftover pizza sauce.

"I like how the middle is still frozen," Sam said. "If you let it rest on your tongue the cold sends rays of cool to your whole head."

"I like this life," I said. "It feels like we're at college."

8

A GREAT IDEA

We painted the chili pot with Destructionator so the whole thing would shine and the evidence of our experiment would disappear.

"My mom will be thanking us night and day," I said.

"Let's Destructionate all her pots," Sam said. "That would totally make up for the blender and spoon incident."

"You know what would beat Destructionating the chili pot?" I asked. "Destructionating our doorknobs."

"Your doorknobs are already shiny," Sam said. "Start with something dirty."

"My mom's tea set is the only filthy thing in our house," I said.

"But that's on the Never Touch list," Sam said.

"Never touch like never make tea in it, which I wouldn't," I said. "Not never touch like never clean it."

I butt-bounced the swinging door open.

The tea set was on the sideboard under the painting with the gold frame.

Sam squatted so he was nose to handle with the teapot.

"Why does your mom like this?" Sam asked.

"Because it's valuable."

"It's cruddy," Sam said.

"Very. But my mom told Aunt Traci that she wouldn't trade it for a thousand dollars."

"It must be like teacups from the *Titanic*," Sam said. "Worn out but worth a lot."

We went through a *Titanic* phase last year.

"Ask your mom how much it's worth," Sam said.

"She says it's rude to ask how much things cost," I said.

"How else are you supposed to find out?" Sam asked.

"Beats me. She did dagger eyes at me when I asked Mrs. Groothousen how much her ring cost. I really wanted to know, because the diamond is the size of my big toenail."

"I bet Mrs. Groothousen gets asked that question night and day," Sam said. "What did she say?"

" 'It's priceless because it's my engagement ring.' "

"That's a useless answer."

"So I said, 'I mean how much is it worth in cash?' That's when my mom interrupted."

"Even if this tea set is only worth a sliver of a diamond ring, we should carry it one piece at a time," Sam said. "For safety and for Operation Zero."

I gave Sam an arm sock of appreciation. "Now, who says we don't plan ahead?"

9

PROTECTING T-POTUS

"We are like Secret Service for this tea set," Sam said. "We'll surround it and protect it at all times."

"If it's in danger, we will throw ourselves in front of it," I said. "Or under it. Depending on if it's robbers or a natural disaster."

"If we're Secret Service, the teapot needs a code name," Sam said. "Like POTUS."

POTUS stands for President of the United States. It's a load quicker for agents to say "POTUS in Oval Office, POTUS eating a ham sandwich, POTUS talking to a king." By the time you say President of the

United States, POTUS could have finished his sandwich and met a king.

"I name thee T-POTUS," I said to the pot.

"You can't name a pot after the president," Sam said.

"I didn't. This POTUS stands for Tea*Pot* and U.S., since we are its agents."

"I like it," Sam said. "For safety we should make T-POTUS a stretcher out of a dish towel and carry it like a sickly patient."

We each took two corners and walked around the table and into the kitchen.

"T-POTUS coming in for a counter landing," Sam said. He has an excellent Secret Service voice.

Then I realized something. "There's only enough Destructionator left to cover T-POTUS's snout."

"I thought that's called a spout," Sam said.

"Don't you remember that kindergarten song 'I'm a little teapot, short and snout'?"

Sam laughed. "All that time I was singing it wrong."

"We have to make a tremendous batch of Destructionator," I said. "It will take a load to clean T-POTUS."

"If we want to surprise your mom—which we do—we better get cracking," Sam said.

I hopped up on the counter so I could reach the top shelf. "I'll get the Tabasco and vinegar," I said. "Pizza sauce is in the pantry."

"Watch it!" Sam said. "You almost kicked T-POTUS."

"Remember OZ," I reminded myself.

"One mistake and it's goodbye, backwards roller coaster," Sam said.

I jumped down and started pouring the leftover Destructionator on T-POTUS's snout when Sam screamed, "Bombs away, Jose!"

Emergency instinct took over my legs. I spun and leapt.

"Got it!" I yelled.

I heard a small pop.

"Was that a bone?" I asked.

"Not this time," Sam said. "I dropped a jar. But no harm, no foul. It hit lid-side down."

"I'm in the catching position," I said.

For a split of a nanosecond it looked like a red banner was flying across the kitchen. Then the sauce fell to the floor.

"Intercept the jar!" Sam yelled. "Block T-POTUS!"

My right leg slid north. My left leg skied south. The jar boomeranged off the fridge and hit the floor.

"You look like a busted wishbone in a river of blood," Sam said.

"Is T-POTUS okay?" I yelled.

Sam made the referee sign for Safe.

"The jar didn't even break," he said.

"Man-o-man alive!" I said. "We are made of pure luck."

I used the drawer handles to pull myself up.

"The floor looks like a giant X-marks-the-spot," I said. "A long red line where sauce landed. And a short red line made by me doing a split."

"Let's put T-POTUS on the table," Sam said. "Like it's on a private island, away from elbows and flying jars."

Who could predict that that was the moment my mom would barge through the back door?

Not me.

10

THE FREAK ACCIDENT

My mother screamed.

Her arms flew out. She stomped straight at me like Frankenstein's monster, only faster, with bendable legs.

"Great-Grandma Sylvia's teapot!" she screamed.

Snatching it unbalanced her. My mom's feet went Fred Flintstone, running but not going anywhere. Then they flew forward. Her arms flew over her head. She was butt-skiing backward. I grabbed her shirt to save her. T-POTUS slipped out of her arms like a live fish.

Sam and I threw ourselves at the

teapot, but it hit the floor. Our heads hit each other. Hard.

The whole time my mom sounded like the McBees' Halloween doormat that makes death noises when trick-or-treaters step on it.

Sam pushed a white kitchen chair across the tile, through the river of sauce. "Sit, Mrs. Melon," he said. "Relax."

She plopped down. I handed over T-POTUS. Her shoulders sank so low they looked boneless. Her eyes looked like dashes. When she talked her lips barely moved. That's a level five hundred on the meter of upsetness.

"Think calm thoughts about starfish, Mom. Or lounging chairs," I said.

"The floor?" she snapped.

"Freak accident," I told her. "Absolutely freak."

She petted the teapot and exhaled. "That's a big dent," she said.

"I've seen bigger," I said. "Remember Mrs. Lee's car?"

"When my dad kicked my globe, the whole Indian Ocean caved in," Sam said. "He said he didn't expect to run into a globe on the steps. Especially in the dark."

"Most dents are acci*dents*," I said. "Get it?"

She did not smile a fraction of a millimeter.

"Don't feel bad, Mrs. Melon," Sam said. "This could happen to anybody."

"It probably has," I said. "To a load of people."

"I cannot imagine who else this could happen to," my mom said. "Except maybe Bart Bigelow."

"Mom!" I said. "Don't compare yourself to a fifth-grade nose-picker who has no self-control."

Her mouth hung open. "Compare *myself*? Do you think that I think the dent is *my* fault?"

"You're the one who dropped the teapot," I said.

"And the one who grabbed it," Sam said. "But who did it isn't important."

"I wouldn't have dropped it if the floor wasn't flooded with tomato sauce," my mom said. "And I wouldn't have snatched it if you hadn't picked it up without permission."

"We were doing you a favor," I said.

"A favor?" my mom said. "Putting tomato sauce on the floor is a favor?"

"The favor is putting it on the teapot," I said.

"And it's pizza sauce on the floor," Sam explained. "The stuff on the teapot is Destructionator."

My mom squeaked. "You put something called Destructionator on Great-Grandma Sylvia's teapot?"

"It wasn't going to put itself on," I said.

I didn't mean to sound flip, but I think I might have out of nervousness.

"Mom," I said. "When you first hear 'Destructionator,' it sounds like a bad thing. It's not. It's a top invention of ours. Believe me. Once you wash the teapot, you will be amazed and thankful."

"Right now I'm amazed and disappointed—in both of you."

That is a sentence I can't stand hearing.

"I'm sorry," I told her.

"Me too," Sam said.

I said what my dad usually says. "Let's put it behind us and move on."

My mom got up.

I turned on the faucet.

"Rinse it off," I said.

"Here comes the big reveal!" Sam said.

Only it didn't.

When my mom finished, the teapot looked exactly like it did when we started. Except for the dent.

11

GREAT-GRANDMA SYLVIA

I stared at the teapot. "Something went wrong," I said.

"Very wrong," my mom said.

"I mean something is wrong with Destruction-ator. The teapot's snout should be shining like tin-foil," I said.

"Spout," my mom said.

"It could be Destructionator only works on some metals," Sam said. "Like copper."

"Shouldn't it work on all metals? Acid is strong stuff," I said.

My mom shrieked. "You've been playing with acid?"

"No," Sam said.

My mom exhaled. "Thank goodness."

"We were working with acid," I said.

"Not the dangerous kind of acid," Sam said.

Her glumness grew.

"Mrs. Melon," Sam said. "Did you ever think you might be overrating the teapot?"

"What?" she said.

"It's not nice-looking," Sam said.

Supersonic brain-to-brain message to Sam: *STOP TALKING!*

"Sam's just saying it was beat-up before the dent. It's got scratches. One leg is bent. It looks old."

"It *is* old," my mom said. "My great-grandma Sylvia gave this teapot to my mother's mother, who left it to my mom, who gave it to me."

"So what you're saying is it's a used teapot," Sam said.

I wanted to ask what made Great-Grandma Sylvia so great, but I thought about my mom's mood. Instead I said, "Mom, did you ever think your teapot might not be worth a thousand bucks?"

"I'd be surprised if it's worth ten dollars," she said.

"That makes sense," Sam said. "It has a cheap look."

"Then why are you upset, Mom? We'll buy you a new teapot that's shiny silver and has more swirls."

My mom stood up, leaned her back against the counter, and closed her eyes for over thirty-five seconds.

"My great-grandmother Sylvia came to New York from Poland when she was twelve years old," she said. "She lived in a tiny apartment with her aunts and uncles and cousins who were already here. It was so crowded that all the girl cousins slept on a mat in the kitchen. In the morning they'd roll it up so people could get in the room."

"Did she live near the Botanical Garden?" Sam asked.

"I don't know," my mom said. "Sylvia worked fourteen hours a day, seven days a week, sewing clothes in a factory that was roasting in the summer and freezing in the winter. She was paid very little money."

"She should've quit," I said.

"In those days it was hard for Polish people to find jobs," my mom said. "A lot of businesses wouldn't hire them."

"Ms. Mad says that's against the law," I said.

"It wasn't then," my mom said. "And Sylvia couldn't quit. The family needed her to help pay the rent and buy food. She saved every penny that was left. After seven years she had enough money to bring her thirteen-year-old sister, Irena, to America."

"On a ship?" Sam asked. "Without her parents?"

My mom nodded.

"Man!" I said. "You would never let me take a boat by myself from Poland to America."

"Irena's mother knew it was the best thing to do," my mom said. "I'm sure she didn't want to let her go."

"Did Irena sleep in the kitchen too?" Sam asked.

"She did. And things got better slowly. The sisters got married and had children. Sylvia's oldest daughter was my mother's mom.

"One day, when they were both old, Irena brought a present to Sylvia. She said it was to thank her for working so hard to give her a life that had made her very happy."

"It was the tea set, right?" I asked.

"Yes," my mom said. "It wasn't the best tea set, but it was the best tea set Irena could afford."

"Was it like it is now?" I asked.

"It was perfect when Irena gave it to her. Sylvia was so proud of that tea set. She used it at parties and celebrations and when guests came over. Her daughters and nieces borrowed it for special occasions. And when the younger cousins got married, Sylvia would shine and pack up the tea set. The morning of the wedding she'd take the bus to St. Stanislaus church and put it in the social hall to use at the reception. When I was little my grandma and I would get dressed up and have tea parties in the sunroom."

"Man-o-man, I'm glad I'm not a girl," I said.

"Ditto," Sam said.

"Ditto," my mom said.

"Do you mean you wish you were a boy?" I asked.

"No," she said. "I mean I'm glad you're a boy."

I felt a little like hugging her.

"Great-Grandma Sylvia's tea set, and especially this teapot, was loved and polished so much that the silver rubbed off in spots. Even if your Destructionator worked on silver, the black patches would still be there."

"We can fix that in a flash," I said. "All we need is silver spray paint."

"You won't even notice the dent when we finish," Sam said.

My mom held up her hand like Mr. Winkle the crossing guard. "Don't start," she said. "The only thing I want fixed is the dent. I like knowing that my family wore it out. The scratches and bare spots make me think about all the people who used it."

"Was your great-grandmother nice?" Sam asked.

"I think she must have been, Sam, but I never met her. She died before I was born."

"How come I never knew this story?" I asked.

"I didn't want you to feel sad, DB," my mom said.

"Why would I be sad?" I asked.

"Of course you're sad," my mom said. "It's a sad story. The family struggled for a long time."

"I think it's a great story," I said. "It's about two sisters who, you know, love each other. Plus, they had adventures and parties. And they got to live with their cousins and sleep on the floor."

"It's about a family that took care of each other," Sam said. "That's a good thing."

"I guess it is," my mom said.

"Probably it backfired sometimes," I said. "Maybe the kid ancestors were cleaning the tea set to surprise their mom and that's how the leg got bent."

"Maybe so," my mom said.

"Mrs. Melon," Sam said.

"What's on your mind, Sam?"

"It's cool how your legs look like they're covered with dried blood," he said.

"That is the most unusual compliment I've ever received," my mom said. "I believe it comes from the heart."

"You're welcome," Sam said.

My mom looked at the kitchen floor. "I'm going upstairs to soak in the tub before my back gets stiff."

"From butt-skiing?" I said.

"Yes," she said. "Afterward I'll come down and clean this kitchen."

"We'll mop up while you're in the tub," Sam said.

"Thank you," she said. "But no. You need hot water. And the floor's slippery."

"Mom, I use hot in the shower sometimes. Also soap. And I don't slip unless I'm trying to."

"You slip on purpose?" she asked.

"Only when I'm pretending to be in a comedy show," I said.

She put her hand on her forehead like she had brain freeze.

"Bathtubs are famous for causing accidents," she said. "No more funny falls."

"It's our personal responsibility to clean up the mess, Mrs. Melon," Sam said.

"It would help a lot if you two would stop walking in the pizza sauce," she said. "Go outside. Hose yourselves clean. Use the ruined beach towels hanging by the basement door."

I disagree that they are ruined, but I was glad she didn't go on about how that happened.

My mom took the teapot upstairs with her.

"That makes me feel like she doesn't trust us," I told Sam.

12

SAM'S SUPREME CLEANING MACHINE

"Incoming BOB," Sam said. "Let's clean it up. When your mom comes back we'll jump out and yell surprise."

Part of me thought of my mom saying don't do it. The other part said, "I'll get the mop."

"Don't need it," Sam said. "You're about to learn the Sam Method. Put these on."

"Oven mittens?"

He pulled our parrot mitt on like a sock.

"Put on the lobster claw," Sam said.

I thought he was going to say, You fell for it.

He didn't. He said, "Do you want the Florida the Sunshine State mitt or What's Cooking, Good-Looking?"

"Florida," I said.

When we both had mitten feet Sam poured Mr. Clean in the yellow bucket and filled it with water.

"Step right in. One foot at a time," he said. "Take it out when it weighs as much as a baby watermelon."

If you've never tried this, it feels like you are standing in pudding.

When Sam finished soaking his feet the bucket was almost empty.

"Now what?" I asked.

"We skate," he said.

He glided through the thickest stripe of sauce.

"E-Z P-Z," I said.

The worst part of Sam's method is that you have to rinse and repeat every few tiles. The best part is sneak attacks. With no warning Sam's parrot slapped my lobster claw.

"Floor war!" Sam said.

"You want a battle, Mc-Faddle?" I said. "My bionic claw has the power of a hundred death grips!"

I flopped my soggy Florida mitt all over his Good-Looking mitt. Also his leg.

"This is a radioactive parrot from an ice cave on the undiscovered planet of Marshmalloni," Sam said. "It weighs seven hundred pounds."

He stomped Florida.

You have to add your own sound effects.

"Mopping is hilarious," I said.

When the fight was done the floor was mostly clean. All we had to do was scrub some dried spots with my toothbrush and skate it dry with four rolls of paper towels.

"Why do people buy mops?" I asked.

"Do you hear footsteps?" Sam asked. "Incoming Mom!"

He fired wet oven mitts at me like baseballs. I threw everything I caught over the back porch railing and slammed the door in the nick of a second.

The kitchen door swung open and we screamed "Surprise!" so loud it was like we had built-in microphones in our necks. My mom looked around like there would be somebody in the kitchen who wasn't Sam or me.

"Who mopped the floor?" she asked.

"We did," I said. "Sam taught me."

"It's clean," she said in the most amazed voice ever.

I could tell she was shocked to the cells inside her bones.

"Did you fall?" she asked.

"Nope," I said. "And don't worry. We used freezing water."

We didn't need hosing off, but we did it anyway. I got the idea of making oven-mitt water balloons and throwing them at each other. They're not as fun as real ones.

When we were pruney we put the mitts on the tomato vine sticks to dry.

While we waited for Sam's dad to pick him up, I made us my famous recipe of dill pickles in taco shells.

"If I don't count the Destructionator, this has been my best food day since Thanksgiving," Sam said.

"From now on the Beast has a three-drop maximum on hot sauce," I said.

"Starting the day after your next turn," Sam said.

13

WHY I NEED AN ALLOWANCE

My dad came home at eleven o'clock that night. He spun my mom around the living room and dipped her down like they were living in the olden days. I'm glad they went out of style.

He hung his jacket on the newel post and headed for the kitchen.

"I'm starving," he said.

I felt bad for not saving him a pickle taco.

"I got you a chocolate almond Twist 'N' Shout at Baking Divas," my mom said.

He gave me the first bite.

My mom gave me a napkin to catch the crumbs.

"Too late," I said.

My mom turned down her bite and had chocolate-cranberry-mousse-flavored Dee-Lite-Full yogurt instead. Bad choice.

"Sit down, Dad," I said. "I'll untie your shoes for you."

"I'm not falling for that again," he said.

"I'm over practical jokes," I said. "Trust me."

"No," he said.

"How was Florida?" my mom asked.

"Fine," he said.

"Did you remember my collection?" I asked.

He took a green-and-white plastic rectangle out of his pocket.

"Thanks," I told him. "Ramada key cards are rare."

"I didn't know that," he said. "Next time I'll ask for an extra. Did anything exciting happen on the home front?"

"Mom dropped her aunt's teapot," I said. "But it was partly Sam's and my fault."

My dad looked dead at me.

"Mostly our fault," I said. "In a way, completely."

"What's the damage?" he asked.

"A dent," my mom said.

He examined the pot.

"We'll get it repaired, Betty. And the boys will pay for it."

"There's a job called dent remover?" I said. "How come I never knew that?"

"We've been keeping that from you," my dad said.

"That's a joke, right?" I asked.

"Yes," my dad said.

"But the part about the dent remover is true?"

"I think so," he said. "We'll have to find a specialist."

"That sounds expensive," my mom said.

"Specialists almost always are," my dad said.

"The boys are awfully young to have to earn money," she said.

"Hard work is good for them, Betty."

"It turns us into men, right, Dad?" I said. "Plus, Sam and I like to work."

"I have a terrific solution!" my mom said. "I'll hire them to do odd jobs."

"The odder, the better," I said.

"That is an expression," she said. "It means you

sweep the porch. Or walk to the post office and mail Grandma's birthday present. In fact, I'll walk with you. I need the exercise."

"Betty," my dad said, "the boys can find their own jobs."

"What if someone wants them to climb a ladder? Or handle toxic chemicals?" my mom said.

My dad put his hand on my shoulder and said, "Promise Mom you won't be a window washer for skyscrapers, Sport."

I hooted. My dad laughed. My mom didn't.

"We'll ask Mrs. Wilkins," I said. "It's impossible to have a freak accident in her house. When she got her fake knee, her daughter put up random railings and ruined the front steps for skateboarding."

"Helping Mrs. Wilkins is always a good idea," my dad said.

"Sam and I are idea guys," I told them.

"Don't get the idea of selling Daddy's ties again," my mom said.

"We could sell the giveaway pile," I said.

"When you and Sam sold the ties-to-keep pile, the giveaways became keepers," my dad said.

"That was a crazy mix-up," I said. "On the good side, your ties are famous now. I see them all over the neighborhood. Mr. Neenobber was wearing the plaid one yesterday. It matched his kilt."

My dad followed me upstairs and stood by the bathroom door while I brushed my teeth. "Sport, was there a way you and Sam could have avoided the teapot situation?" he asked.

"Can we call it something else?" I asked. "Sam and I are trying to get away from incidents and situations."

"You may call it what you like," he said.

"I'd like to call it a snafu," I said.

"Okay," he said. "What did you learn from the snafu?"

"That Destructionator doesn't clean silver."

"Did you remember the Guideline for Life that says If in Doubt Ask an Adult?"

"Sure," I said. "But we weren't in doubt."

"How about Think Before Doing?" my dad asked.

"We did think," I said. "What we thought was when Mom sees her shining teapot she'll do a hula from happiness."

"How about Ask Permission Before You Touch Someone's Belongings?" my dad said.

"That's not a G for L," I said.

"It is now," he said.

I was lying in bed chewing year-old Sour Patch Kids that I found under my radiator when I got an idea about how to make them soft again. I crept down the hall to the bathroom and filled my toothbrush cup with water. On my way back I heard my parents talking in their bedroom. I flattened myself against the wall like a spy.

Eavesdropping on my parents is one of my hobbies.

"How do the boys think of these ideas?" my mom said.

My dad's voice is louder. "I know it seems goofy, Betty. But some things are irresistible to boys. When I was ten my brother and I had a fight with the silver candlesticks my mom keeps on top of the piano."

"At least the candlesticks were already wobbly," my mom said. "My teapot was dent-free."

My dad laughed. "Betty, before the War of the Melon Brothers, those candlesticks were as straight as rulers."

"I don't give your mother enough credit," my mom said.

"Don't worry about our boy," my dad told her. "He and Sam are smart kids."

"You're saying they do odd things because they're so bright?" she asked. "Of course. Why didn't I realize that?"

She had some of her old Mom zip back.

"Now you can relax," my dad said.

"Of the two, I'd say Adam is the smarter," my mom said.

"I'd say we don't have to compare their brains," he told her.

"Tomorrow I'll call Dr. Stroud and let him know that Adam is even more intelligent than we thought."

"I'd hold off on that, Betty," my dad said.

"As a doctor he'll want to make a note on Adam's chart," my mom said. "Dr. Stroud probably has special advice for the parents of gifted children."

"You're a good mom, Betty," my dad said.

14

BIG BOB

It turns out that soaking Sour Patch Kids in water does not make them soft. It makes them slimy, which is good if you want to stick wet Kids under your top lip so you look like you have jewels for teeth. Bite their heads into points. It's funnier that way.

I couldn't fall asleep until I thought up a way to make dent-removing money. Once I did I was too excited to sleep. But I must have closed my eyes because I woke up and it was seven a.m.

I ran into my parents' room and picked up my mom's sleeping mask.

"I need to go to Sam's," I said

"That's fine, once you're dressed and you've

brushed your teeth," my mom said. "Help Mrs. Alswang with Baby Julia."

"Okay."

"Don't eat them out of house and home, DB."

"I won't."

I got there fast. I had to lean on the Alswangs' doorbell for a long time. Sometimes they're slow to get out of bed. I hollered through the mail slot, "Hello in there! It's me, Melonhead."

"It's open!" Sam's mom yelled. "We're in the kitchen."

Baby Julia was sitting on the counter soaking her legs in the sink, which was full of bubble water, and salting her knees. Mrs. Alswang was washing her neck. Julia's, I mean. Not her own.

"Behwinhid," Julia said. "Serull."

"Julia knows my pockets are always stuffed with cereal," I told Mrs. Alswang.

"Except for at weddings," Sam said.

"My mom made that rule after I was the ring carrier at my cousin Kate's wedding."

"Something happened?" Mrs. Alswang asked.

"It wasn't his fault," Sam said.

"Nobody told me rental pants have crummy pockets that scooch up when you walk," I said. "Plus, Kate told me keep your eyes on the rings."

"Because they're made of solid gold," Sam told his mom.

"How was I supposed to I know I was leaving a trail of Froot Loops?" I asked.

Mrs. Alswang laughed.

"Fluloo," Julia said.

"Was the bride upset?" Mrs. Alswang asked.

"She said I saved the day. The flower girl forgot to drop petals. Thanks to me, the bride had something colorful to walk on."

Julia held out her hand. "Fluloo."

Mrs. Alswang said she could have Cheerios. I gave

her some from the cabinet. She squeezed them into wet mush with one hand and kept salting her legs with the other. Julia, not Mrs. Alswang. That would be ridiculous.

"Sam, please give your sister her Daddy doll in exchange for the salt shaker."

Daddy doll is Sam's old GI Joe wearing girl doll leopard-spot pants. If I were Mr. Alswang I would not feel complimented.

Julia was so excited to see Daddy doll she dropped the saltshaker in the water.

"Time for a meeting," I told Sam.

"To the trunk room," Sam said.

Over one hundred years ago, when Sam's house was built and before suitcases caught on, houses came with little rooms so people had a place to keep their trunks. Mr. Alswang turned theirs into an office.

I explained my plan.

"BOB times infinity!" Sam shouted.

"We'll make so much money we can get the teapot fixed and buy my mom a Jet Ski for a make-up present," I said.

Sam plopped down in the spinning chair. "I'll type."

I sat on top of one of the file cabinets. There's another chair but I like heights.

WE-FIX-IT COMPANY

You break it, we fix it.

You lose it, we find it. (Usually.)

You want it, we get it.

You buy it, we haul it.

You grow it, we mow it.

You need it, we build it.

We set up an email address for the We-Fix-It Company.

While Sam waited for the flyers to come out of the printer, I sent a message.

> Dear Aunt Traci & Uncle Ben,
>
> We are on Day Five of OZ. So far, zero situations. We did have one snafu. Get ready for the rides of your lives.
>
> Your nephew and his friend,
> Melonhead & Sam

We had to take all the photos off Mr. Alswang's bulletin board to get enough thumbtacks to hang our flyers.

"First stop: Madam and Pop's," I said.

They are our most loyal bosses.

"I'm ready, Freddy," Sam said.

He reached behind his ear. Then he looked at the floor.

"Do you see my gum?"

"It's not in your hair?" I asked.

"No. I think the last place I saw it was on the back of my hand."

I crawled under the desk. "It's not here. When was the last time you noticed it?"

"Before you got here. I put it on my hand so I could eat tomato sandwiches," he said.

Tomato and mayonnaise sandwiches are Sam's top breakfast.

"My detecting senses are telling me to look in the kitchen," I said.

Luckily, Mrs. Alswang and Julia had moved to the living room to have a dancing session.

"If it's gone all that chewing is wasted," Sam said.

"Just start over," I said.

"I'm not enjoying gum these days," he said.

"I did not know that was possible," I said.

We looked in the basement.

"At least it's not in the dryer," Sam said. "Remember when that happened? Your mom was so popping mad she called your dad at work."

"To be fair to me, I had no idea she was going to wash my pants," I said. "If I had, I would not have left my personal gum collection in my pocket."

"I never knew gum could melt until I saw it stretched all over your clothes," Sam said. "And the insides of the dryer."

"Here's what I think about your gum," I said. "As long as you find and chew it before midnight, you are still in the contest."

15

JOB ONE

We skateboarded down Independence Avenue yelling, "Workers for hire! Get your red-hot workers!"

"Everybody looks at the Grubb's drugstore community news wall," Sam said.

We hung our flyer between Free Kittens and Guitar Lessons in Your Home.

A lady tapped my shoulder. "Tell your bosses We-Fix-It is exactly what this neighborhood needs."

She turned away before I could say we were the bosses.

The people at Congress Market hung it by the meat case.

"So far, so easy," I said.

We crossed at the light near Madam and Pop's house.

"Take the shortcut," Sam said.

He flipped over Madam and Pop's fence and landed on his feet. I landed on the pansies. Sometimes it's the other way around.

They were sitting on the side porch.

Pop called our shortcut a remarkable time-saver. Then he told Madam, "You would be a marvelous fence jumper."

Madam rolled her eyes like Pop was the mayor of Crazytown.

Then Pop said, "I hate to see talent wasted. If you work hard and we get you a coach, you could be ready for the next Olympics."

I told him the bad news from Wikipedia.

"There is no such thing as Olympic fence jumping, Pop."

"They canceled it?" he said.

Then he put his hands on Madam's shoulders and said, "This is a big stumbling block, my dear. Without the Olympics it's unlikely you'll be able to turn fence jumping into a career."

"I can always compete at the amateur level," Madam said.

"That's the attitude," Pop told her. "Keep your sunny side up."

Madam laughed.

"Climb up here and have some fruit, boys," she said.

The water meter makes a good ladder.

"What's the scoop du jour?" Pop said.

"Guess," Sam said.

We always say that because Pop is the King of Jokers.

He leaned forward in his porch chair and put his chin on his fist like that statue of that man. I can't remember what it's called. He looks like he's thinking.

"I've got it," Pop said. "The school system is finally teaching fifth graders to drive."

"I wish," I said. "I'd drive the

footpool every day. If I had a car, I mean."

"Surely the District of Columbia school system would not expect fifth graders to buy their own cars," Pop said.

"They would," Sam said.

"What do we pay taxes for if not to buy cars for children?" Pop asked Madam.

"Sit down, boys," Madam said.

I sat but I bounced back up the minute my butt hit the railing.

I yowled. Sam howled.

"My back pocket is full of thumbtacks," I said.

Even Madam laughed, and she's the one who has sympathy.

Sam handed over a We-Fix-It flyer and sat with one leg on each side of the railing. I stood and picked cherries out of the bowl.

"Open wide, Hyde," I said.

The cherry bounced off Madam's eyebrow.

"Sorry," I said.

"What does We-Fix-It fix?" Pop asked.

"Anything that's busted," Sam said.

"Plus, we do chores," I said. "One dog walked for one dollar. Ten walks a day during the week. Thirty or more walks on the weekends."

"Gumbo is not a reliable dog," Pop said. "Especially when she sees a squirrel."

Sam poked his pointer finger through the middle of a clementine. "For six dollars we'll cook your dinner," he said.

"Tempting," Pop said. "But we're still rich in cheese cubes."

"They came from the Cranberry Growers reception," Sam said.

"Do you have anything that needs to be covered with tar?" I asked.

"I don't believe we do," Madam said.

"Wait one minute," Pop said. "Are you saying you don't mind messy, sticky, smelly work?"

"That's our best kind," I said.

"Wait here," he said.

Pop came back with a pair of sneakers. The bottoms were peeled like bananas. Tan rubber was hanging from the heels.

"Shoe flaps," I said.

"I knew you'd understand the problem," Pop said. "And I'm glad you came by. I was about to throw  these away. Can you reglue the soles?"

"In my sleep," I said.

"You'll need special glue," Madam said. "You can charge it to our account at Frager's Hardware."

"Save your money," Sam said. "We have every glue ever made. My dad is a supply guy."

"How much will this repair cost?" Pop asked.

"Is seven dollars too much?" I asked. "Three dollars per shoe plus a dollar for delivery."

"I'll pay you in advance, if that's okay," Pop said.

"That's tremendously okay," Sam said.

"Your shoes are in good hands," I told Pop.

I wasn't trying to be funny, but when I heard myself I laughed like a pelican.

"I'm having some young people over for tea today," Madam said. "Is it possible the Fix-It men could pick up my order at Baking Divas?"

"Hot diggity dog in a bog," I told her. "Baking Divas is our top store on Capitol Hill."

"Triple win," Sam said. "We make money and pass out flyers, and Mrs. McBee might give us a day-old cookie for free."

Mrs. McBee is our friend Jonique's mom. She is one of the Divas. Mrs. McBee, I mean. Jonique is too young to be a diva.

"I need eight Blue Plate Specials," Madam said.

"The Divas are serving specials?" I asked. "Like at the Tastee Diner?"

"Like meat loaf and pork chops?" Sam asked.

"I have no idea what's on the menu, but Mrs. McBee told me the specials are her greatest triumph," Madam said.

"I say the Divas should stick with sweets and sandwiches," Sam said.

"I already asked Mrs. McBee to put it on our account," Madam said. "Tell her that I said you can each pick a treat."

I cannot wait to get accounts.

"Thanks, Madam and Pop," I said.

We were dead shocked when we turned the corner on Seventh Street. The line to get in to the Divas went out the door and past Acqua 2 restaurant. Our friend Justin is a busboy there. That's one of our dream jobs.

"What's going on?" Sam said.

A skinny lady with a double stroller said, "Everyone wants a Blue Plate."

"Who knew they'd be so popular? Not me."

"I'll be the placeholder in line," I told Sam. "You hand out flyers in Eastern Market."

He came back ten minutes later.

"I gave every one of the Canales brothers a flyer and two to the people at the booth that sells raw chicken feet," he said.

"I'd eat one on a dare," I said.

"A chicken foot or a flyer?" Sam asked.

"Either one," I said. "But I would only brag about the foot."

"I touched one," Sam said. "It felt like wet rubber. In a creepy way."

Sam stayed in line. I went to the Diva Dog Hitching Post in front of the store. The Rosens' dog licked my eyebrows. It makes you feel like your eyeballs are being spun.

A girl named Zoe who's in sixth grade saw me and said, "Melonhead, dog spit in your eye is gross and unrefined."

"It's just nature," I said.

16
TAKE A NUMBER

Jonique's Diva aunt Frankie has not let Sam and me pick a Take a Number to Be Served ticket since the time we took twenty-two numbers. Today everybody had to take a number. I was 67. Sam was 66.

"Melonhead! Sam!"

Lucy Rose and Jonique were behind the counter.

"How come you guys get to fold boxes?" Sam asked.

"It's all hands on deck," Aunt Frankie said.

"We'll get on deck," I told her.

"Thanks anyway," Aunt Frankie said.

Lucy Rose was standing on a step stool, holding her arms wide like a prize lady

on *The Price Is Right.*
"In this glass case be-
fore you are the Blue
Plate Specials!"

Sam and I pressed
our foreheads against
the glass and looked
at masterpieces.

"Mrs. McBee created the whole beauteous thing,"
Lucy Rose said. "*Beauteous* is my Word of the Day. It
means 'so beautiful it's stunning.'"

"They're like a real dinner, only sweet and minia-
turized!" Jonique said. "You pick one meat and two
sides."

"Are they food or cookies?" I asked.

"Cookies are food," Aunt Frankie said.

"These hamburgers are actually tiny cakes," Mrs.
McBee told everybody in line. "This tiny chicken
drumstick is a caramel spice cookie. The broccoli is
an iced butter cookie."

"That's my kind of vegetable," I said.

"They're like doll food," number 70 said. "You
can see every kernel of the corn on the cob."

"The corn makes me proud of myself," Jonique's mom told number 70. "I took a can of baby corn ears to Baltimore Metal Crafters and Mr. Phillips cast those little ears in aluminum. He made us a pan with forty corn impressions. We fill them with sweet corn cake batter and bake for four minutes."

"We glaze them so they look buttered," Aunt Frankie said.

"What other vegetables does Mr. Phillips make?" I asked.

"Baby corn was his first," Mrs. McBee said.

"Make way for mashed potatoes and hot dogs," Mr. McBee said.

Mr. McBee's job is keeping track of the government's money. Usually he only works at the bakery when Hanukkah and Christmas come during the same week.

"We're picking up for Madam," Sam told him.

"She phoned in her order early this morning," Mrs. McBee said. "We were set to deliver, but, bless her heart, she just called back to say you'd be picking it up. I couldn't be more grateful. I've got two delivery people and thirty-two boxes waiting to go."

"Do you want us to deliver?" I asked.

"Can you drop this box off at the Blossoms' on your way back to Madam and Pop's?" Mrs. McBee asked.

"You bet," I said.

Aunt Frankie started filling a white box for Madam. "Carrots, pork chops, burgers, french fries, a banana."

"Look at the banana split," I said. "It's a dessert disguised as another dessert."

"Don't forget a mini-cherry pie," Sam said.

"It only took one cherry to make it," Jonique said.

I picked a piece of pizza for my one thing on Madam and Pop's account. Sam got a fried egg. The middle was a yellow M&M.

Jonique gave us eight small paper plates. They were white with blue edges.

"Here's eight mini-napkins," Lucy Rose said, "folded by me until my fingers were utterly exhausted."

"This Blue Plate is for you two for delivering the Blossoms' Doughnutty Buddies," Jonique said.

Sam and I crossed the street to Eastern Market so we could be in the shade. We sat on the curb next to the flower lady and scarfed down our shrunken food.

When we got to the Blossoms' house I yelled "Special delivery!" so loud baby Desmond woke up.

When we got back to Madam and Pop's and they opened the Baking Divas box, they were gobsmacked. *Gobsmacked* comes from England. Hannah in our class says it a lot. It means "shocked times infinity."

"I'm going to eat an ear of corn," Madam said.

Pop picked a sausage.

They traded bites to double the experience.

"Madam," Sam said. "You have sausage stuck to your teeth."

She snapped her lips shut.

"Don't worry," I said. "It looks cool. Like you have rotting zombie teeth."

Pop said, "You continue to have a way with the ladies, Melonhead."

"I feel like I'm getting better at understanding them," I said.

Madam went inside. When she came back the sausage was gone.

"If you don't like colorful teeth eat the mashed potato cookies," Sam said.

"I don't know if I can get used to eating mashed potatoes with my hands," Madam said.

"It's easy," I said. "I've done it loads of times."

"Ditto," Sam said.

"I meant mashed potatoes, the cookie," Madam said.

"Oh, you'll be used to that even faster," I said.

Madam gave Sam and me five dollars for picking up and delivering.

"Counting the shoe money and the tip from Mrs. Blossom, we have twelve dollars and seventy-five cents," I said.

"This is the speediest money on earth," Sam said.

17

PIP

We met up with Pip by accident. Not the crashing kind. We were leaving Madam and Pop's. She was coming from Stanton Park.

"Why are you guys here?" she asked.

"For a snack and shoe pickup," I said.

"You just hop in any old time and beg for food and shoes?" she asked.

"Just food," Sam said.

"We don't beg," I said. "They just give it to us."

"We used to hint around when we first met them," Sam said. "But Madam said be direct."

"Now we directly ask," I told her.

"I'm dropping off carrot muffins," Pip said.

"Sometimes we bring them cheese," I told her.

"The muffins are a thank-you for Pop helping my dad hang shelves in Merrie's room," Pip said. "My sister Meredith is the baker, so they're good. You should beg directly for one."

"Beg Pop or Meredith?" I asked.

"You'll have better luck with Pop," she said.

"I would only eat carrot muffins if my other choice was liver paste," Sam said. "No offense."

"Meredith calls them muffins," Pip said. "But my mom says, 'Why pretend? Muffins are cupcakes for breakfast.'"

"Which do they taste like?" I asked.

"Cupcakes," she said.

"We'll ask Pop directly," Sam said.

"Do you want to help us hang We-Fix-It flyers?" I asked. "We're the owners and fixers."

"That depends on if Lucy Rose is here," Pip said.

Luckily, she wasn't.

Pip talked to Madam and Pop from the sidewalk.

I jumped back over the fence and handed up the cupcake-muffins.

"Thank you," Madam said.

Before I could ask she gave us one to split.

"Pip?" Madam said.

"I ate one on the way here," she said.

"Then you must have a pork chop," Pop said.

"Now?" Pip asked.

I passed a mini-chop over the fence.

"I wish you could eat real pork chops in one bite," she said.

"I wish real pork chops were cookies," Sam said.

"Who doesn't," I said.

18

WE NEED CUSTOMERS

"Put Pop's shoes in my backsack so your hands will be free for flyers," Pip said.

A backsack is like a backpack, only it goes across the back of Pip's wheelchair. One of her sisters made it out of stretchable string.

"We should hand out Fix-It signs near Watkins Elementary School," Pip said. "People with kids always have broken stuff."

"Smart," I said.

"Also in front of Frager's," she said.

"Not smart," Sam said. "People who buy stuff at hardware stores already know how to fix stuff. They don't need us."

"Wrong," Pip said. "Lots of people buy supplies before they find out they can't do the job. Like my dad and the shelves."

"Well then, hello, easy money!" Sam said.

I waved myself around like I was easy money walking down the street.

"You're great at business, Pip," I said.

"It's one of my natural abilities," she said.

In Florida, where I used to live, the hardware store is one gigantic building. In the city, it's lots of skinny buildings stuck together.

Pip borrowed a yard of duct tape from Frager's.

"Give it to me," I said. "I have built-in scissors. They're called canine teeth."

"Dr. Bowers says don't use your teeth for tearing," Pip said.

"He has no way of knowing," I said.

"I bet they learn how to spot scissor teeth in dentist school," Sam said.

"It's possible," I said. "He knows when I skip flossing my teeth."

"Because you never floss," Sam said.

"I have to save the floss for

important things," I said. "Like tying flashlights to my head."

"That took a load of floss," Sam said.

"It was worth it," I said. "How else can you see all the way to the bottom of strangers' trash cans and keep your hands free for picking out the good stuff?"

"Does the word *disgusting* mean anything to you?" Pip asked.

We taped flyers to the lampposts and thumbtacked them to the trees in front of Frager's and the Garden Center and the Rent-It-All.

"I'll give them to customers who look unhandy," Pip said.

Guess who she picked first? Dr. Bowers.

Two things. 1. It's spooky times infinity that he popped up right after we were talking about him. 2. How could Pip think he was unhandy? If you can fix teeth, you can fix anything.

Dr. Bowers put the flyer in his pocket and hopped on his bike. "See you in six months or less," he said. "And, Melonhead, stop using your teeth for scissors."

"He knows things," I said.

19

ONE MAN'S TREASURE

"Let's take the Sixth Street alley home," I said.

"Nothing happens in alleys," Pip said.

"You're as wrong as a sour milk shake," I said.

"We get our best supplies in alleys," Sam said.

"We found a doorbell in the Keenans' trash," I said. "Do you know how much they cost at Frager's? A lot."

"Does it work?" Pip asked.

"Probably," I said. "It's got wires sticking out of the back."

"A might-work doorbell is not worth digging around in trash for," Pip said.

"Maybe not to you," Sam said.

"It's not just the doorbell," I said. "Pop thinks the

stuff we rescued is so great he calls it Another Man's Treasure."

"We got a six-inch bolt and tiles we can use when we build our space shuttle," Sam said.

"One trash can," Pip said. "That's all I'm trying."

"Deal," I said. "Follow me. We'll start with Senator Lavin's trash. The Lavins are remodeling their bathroom."

"I do not want somebody's used toilet," Pip said.

"If there is a toilet, we have first dibs," I said. "It's one of our top wishes."

"The Lavins have four daughters," Sam said. "There's probably some good girl stuff in their trash."

"Not like stuff for good girls," I said. "Good stuff for regular girls."

"The Lavin sisters are good," Pip said. "Last year at school Ellie got the prize for Most Thoughtful."

I took the lid off and told her, "Take your pick, Pip."

"I choose the black garbage bag with the plug hanging out," she said.

"Plugs are usually attached to something interesting," Sam said.

She pulled the cord up like she was crabbing.

"I have always wanted a light-up plastic elf!" she yelled.

"How did you know they existed?" I asked.

"How did you not know?" Pip said.

Sam spotted binoculars.

"One lens is cracked," Pip said.

"That's okay," Sam said. "I'll keep one eye shut."

By the end of the Lavins' trash Pip's backsack was sagging from a hunk of plaster. She said she was going to carve it to look like her mom. The elf had to ride on her lap.

"When I think how I almost missed the telescoping ceiling duster, my stomach clamps tight," I said.

"If I hadn't tried to grab it from you we'd never know it stretched," Sam said.

"What are you going to dust?" Pip asked.

"We're going to use it to invent a weapon," I said.

"Or hook it up to a camera," Sam said. "The FBI could sneak it through windows when they need to spy on crooks."

"That's a BOB, Sam," I said.

"Who's Bob?" Pip asked.

"BOB stands for Brainflash of Brilliance," I said. "It's a good thing."

"I have time for one more trash hunt," Pip said. "Then I have to get ready for Jonique's sleepover party."

"I vote for Jimmy T's," Sam said. "We've never found bad trash there."

"Let's roll," Pip said.

We waited until there were zero cars on East Capitol Street so we could stop for a second in the middle and have one foot in Northeast Washington and the other foot in Southeast Washington. Pip braked on the dividing line, so her feet were in SE while the rest of her was in NE. Being in two places at once sounds more exciting than it is, but we still like to do it.

At Jimmy T's, Pip parked so close to the Dumpster that the side of her chair touched the bin. Then she locked the brakes, pulled on her racing gloves, and made herself the boss.

"Melonhead, we'll boost you up. I'll be your right foot stirrup," she said. "Sam, you're the left."

Sam weaved his fingers together.

"Ready, set, hoist," Pip said.

I stepped in.

"You're heavier than you were last week," Sam said.

"Put your right foot in my hand," Pip told me.

"Ready, steady, lift," Sam said.

The leg on Pip's side went up faster and smoother than Sam's leg. I mean my leg that Sam was in charge of. It's impossible to boost up your own legs.

I folded my stomach over the side of the Dumpster and leaned in.

"Who wants a giant cardboard Coca-Cola bottle?" I yelled.

"Not me," Sam said.

"I do," Pip said.

I tossed it over.

"I'm going to tape it to my wall sideways so it'll look like it's about to spill," she said.

You have to admit, Pip has ideas.

"There's something in a clear bag," I said. "It's buried. I have to pull it out."

I yanked.

"This isn't trash," I said.

"What isn't?" Pip asked.

"It's a tube of little plastic tubs. With lids. The carry-out kind that get filled with sauce," I said. I threw them over the side

All of a sudden Pip gave the bottom of my right

foot a tremendous shove straight up. My head smash-landed on an ice cream bucket. It didn't smell bad.

"You dumped me on purpose!" I yelled.

"Stay down. Mr. T's coming," Pip hissed.

"That's okay," I said from my trash heap. "He's our good friend."

"He looks steaming mad," Pip said.

"Sam! Melonhead!"

Mr. T has a sonic boom of a voice.

"Yes," I said.

I was trying to stand up but the trash kept sink-ing. Mr. T grabbed the back of my cargo shorts and my T-shirt and lifted me up with my butt in the air. Having the top of my shorts pushing against my guts made my voice squeak like I was a cartoon character.

"This is how a spider feels when it's hanging by a thread," I said. "Except the spider owns the thread, so he knows where he's going to land. I don't."

"You kids should not be going through my trash."

"We're not allowed in your trash?" Sam asked.

"Nobody told us," I said. "Really. They never did."

Mr. T dropped me on my feet.

"We were looking for cool stuff," Pip said.

"I don't throw away cool stuff," Mr. T said.

"You throw away heaps of cool stuff," Sam said.

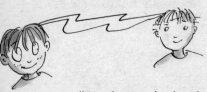 Supersonic brain-to-brain message to Sam: *Stop before he figures out that this is not our first time in his trash bin.*

"So this isn't the first time you kids have invaded my trash," he said.

Never mind.

"It's Pip's first time," I said. "I was the one who said we should come here."

"Did you think it might be against my rules?" Mr. T asked.

"No," I said.

"Never," Sam said.

"I did," Pip said. "Nobody wants people in their trash."

"You thought that?" Sam asked.

"Mr. T, I thought it was fine because we're friends," I said.

"We are friends," Mr. T said. "I would care a whale of a lot if you got hurt."

That seemed like a weak excuse.

"If Melonhead hadn't checked on your trash he couldn't have rescued your plastic mini-cups," Sam said.

"I threw them away," Mr. T said. "We ordered the wrong size. Too big for ketchup, too small for slaw."

"But you could put buttons in them," Pip said. "Or M&M's."

"Too risky," Mr. T said. "I might get them confused."

Suddenly a huge laugh burst out of him.

That was a sign. He was over being mad.

"May I keep the cups?" Pip asked.

"Consider them a souvenir of the last time you three will touch my trash."

She thanked Mr. T like owning cups was the great dream of her life.

"Pip, I'm starting to think you're the ringleader," Mr. T said. "Boys will do some knuckleheaded things for a pretty girl."

I could feel redness sliding down my face like liquid grease. Sam was the opposite. Snow-white. Not the fairy-tale lady. The color.

"Oh, come on, boys," Mr. T said. "How do you think I charmed Mrs. T into marrying me?"

I sneak-looked at Pip. Her face was almost purple.

"We're sorry, Mr. T," I said.

"Very," Sam said.

"All right," he said. "Wash your hands when you get home."

"Melonhead always has sanitizer," Pip said.

"Only because my mom makes me," I said.

As soon as Mr. T left, Pip said, "I am not ringleading anybody."

"How could he think what he thought?" I asked.

I coasted down Fifth Street with my face blazing hot. That happens when I'm dead embarrassed. It didn't stop until Pip's turnoff.

"I've got to go," Pip said. "Don't forget Pop's shoes."

I hardly got them out of her backsack before she peeled off. Halfway down the block she turned around and yelled.

"Do you guys really know how to do the jobs on the Fix-It flyer?"

"Mostly," I hollered.

"We learn fast!" Sam shouted.

20

HOUSE OF ACTION

Sam let us in with the key from his neck chain.

"Why is Julia lying on her back kicking like a bug?" I asked.

"She enjoys it," Sam said.

"Yi yi," Julia said.

"Hello, bug," I said.

"Fffftt," Julia said.

"Was that an insult?" I asked.

"I think so," Sam said.

"Hello, boys," Mrs. Alswang said. She was in the living room, standing on a red chair, holding a broom with a sock on the top end. She was poking the ceiling.

"I like coming into a house of action," I told her.

"Thank you," Mrs. Alswang said. "Considering how flimsy cobwebs are, you'd think I could get them down in one swipe."

"I wouldn't think that. Cobwebs have to be sticky," I said.

"Icky," Julia said.

"Otherwise bugs would bounce off and the spiders would starve," I said. "You can borrow our telescoping duster. It's on your porch."

"Do you always travel with a duster?" Mrs. Alswang asked.

"Just today," Sam said.

"I'm relieved to hear that," Mrs. Alswang said.

"Can we go on the computer?" Sam asked.

"Don't get sucked into a game," Mrs. Alswang said. She thinks computer games are a waste.

We ran up the steps two at a time.

"We got Fix-It mail!" Sam said.

"Read it out loud," I told him.

"Dear We-Fix-It Company,

Do you build birdhouses? I'd like to
get one made for my wife's birthday.
Could you send me a price estimate?

Thank you,
George E. West"

"Hot diggity, wiggity dog!" I said. "Welcome, customer number one."

Sam typed.

Dear Mr. West,

We do. They cost $6.

Sincerely,
The We-Fix-It Company

*****

Dear Sirs,

Our yard needs pruning. Do you
have experience with crape myrtles
and Swedish ivy? We'll be visiting
Lancaster, Pennsylvania, for two
days, starting tomorrow. I can meet
with you any morning after that.

Hilary Benson

"Problem: the Bensons might fire us once they find out we're the Fix-It men," Sam said. "They still blame us for the car-washing snafu."

"If glass wasn't clear it would be easier to tell when a window was open," I said.

"True," Sam said. "By now they probably realize that they overreacted."

"Let's tell Mrs. Benson that we have to do the job while they're in Pennsylvania," I said. "They can mail us our pay when they get back."

"I like how you think, Stink."

"I'm a Fix-It guy, Pie."

While I was typing our answer to Mrs. Benson, we got more mail.

Dear We-Fix-It Company,

I would like the birdhouse to be round and rustic. It should blend in with nature and must be waterproof. My wife's birthday is in three days. It must be delivered on time. Six dollars is a reasonable price. Please proceed.

With appreciation,
George E. West

"What's *rustic?*" Sam asked.

We looked it up. Also *proceed.*

Then we did enough high fives to equal high eighty.

```
Dear Mr. George E. West,

We will build your wife a plain,
simple, natural, outdoor-looking
birdhouse. We will start, or as you
say, proceed, tomorrow.

Thank you for the work,
The We-Fix-It Company
```

"My mind is boggled by our success," Sam said.

"Boggled times amazed times infinity," I said.

Boggled is one of Lucy Rose's Words of the Day. It means "overwhelmed and astonished."

I called my mom to check if Sam could come for dinner.

"If he has permission," my mom said.

"He does," I said. "We already asked."

When we got to my house my dad was setting the table.

"Hello, Sport," he said. "Good to see you, Sam. Any snafus today?"

"Not even a snaf," I said.

We were eating salad when my mom said, "Honey, did you track down a dent remover yet?"

"I asked around at the office," my dad said. "Oddly, no one has had this problem before."

"There's a guy in Baltimore," I said.

"His name is Mr. Phillips," Sam said. "And by the way, dent removers are actually called metalsmiths."

"Really?" my dad said.

"We wouldn't kid you about a metalsmith, Dad."

"I'll be amazed if Mr. Phillips the Metalsmith can fix it," my mom said.

"Mom, if he can make baby corn, he can do anything," I said.

"I don't know what that means," my mom said.

"It means we're going to Baltimore this week," my dad told her.

"State testing starts tomorrow morning," my mom said. "School gets out at noon."

"This is a light work week for me," my dad said. "I can take off after lunch."

"Am I going to Baltimore too?" Sam asked. "Please? Remember, Mr. Melon. I am part of the problem."

"That you are, Sam," my dad said. "I'll talk to your parents."

"Unless going to Baltimore is private family time," Sam said. "If it is, my mom says I have to be aware and not hang around."

"At times like these I think of you like a son, Sam," my dad said.

"Thanks," Sam said.

The phone rang during dishwasher loading. We were finished by the time my mom hung up.

"Who was it?" my dad asked.

"My sister. Traci wanted to know if Adam and Sam had gotten into any situations."

"That's strange," my dad said.

My mom shook her head. "I can tell she wants to get me to Transform DB."

"She doesn't give up," my dad said.

"What did you tell her?" I asked.

"I changed the subject," my mom said.

"Good for you, Mom."

Supersonic b-to-b message to Sam: *Double relief.*

I could tell Sam was sending the same message back.

My parents went to sit on the back porch to drink coffee and what was left of the Dream Cream. Sam and I charged upstairs.

"Where's your sock full of Jolly Ranchers?" Sam asked.

"In my underwear drawer," I said. "Only now I have four socks half-full. I divided by flavor."

"Give me the blue sock, please," Sam said.

I threw it backward over my shoulder.

"You got me dead in the head, Ned."

"Mistake, Jake," I said.

"No big deal, Banana Peel."

"We still have to glue Pop's shoe," I said.

"Come over early tomorrow," Sam said. "Before school."

My dad yelled up the stairs. "Sam! Your father's here."

"Coming!" he yelled.

My mom's against banister sliding, so we took the longcut down the stairs. Mr. Alswang and my dad were talking about Baltimore.

Julia was sitting on the rug, but when she saw me she lay down on her belly.

"She wants to play grocery cart," I said. "That's when I pick up her legs and Sam puts food on her back. Light food only. She's too little to carry a ham."

"It's Julia's favorite game," Mr. Alswang said. "Invented by your brilliant son."

"I'm just realizing how brilliant he is," my mom said. "I've been unable to keep the slugs from raiding my garden, but he invented the solution."

"I did?"

"What do you call them, DB? I call them slug ghosts because that's what they look like."

Supersonic emergency message: What is she talking about?

Sam had no idea either. "Slug ghosts?" he asked.

"When did you put my oven mitts on sticks in the garden?" my mom asked.

"Last night," I said.

"This morning, no slugs. No holes in the lettuce," my mom said. "The mittens must be like a scarecrow for slugs."

"Pop says your son's mind works in interesting ways," Mr. Alswang said. "And from what I've seen, Pop is right."

"Pop was one of the first to recognize how gifted and talented Adam is," my mom said.

"Just like Sam," my dad said. "The boys are equally smart."

"We invented the slug ghosts together," I said.

"We'll take Julia into the kitchen," Sam said. "That's where the groceries are."

"Tell me more about this brilliant game Adam invented," my mom said to Mr. Alswang.

Sam picked his sister up. "What's wrong with her hair, Dad?"

"She has a gum nest," Mr. Alswang said.

"Julia got gum in her hair?" Sam asked.

"That's terrible!" my mother said, like gum was a nuclear accident.

"Linda hasn't seen it yet," Sam's dad said. "She'll be unhappy. But I say when you're as pretty as Julia, you can afford a bald spot."

We went into the kitchen and Sam put his sister down on the floor.

"Well, we found your gum," I said.

"Goom," Julia said.

Sam opened our bread box.

"Bagel," he said.

Julia threw the bagel.

"I could go for some defrosted potato skins about now," Sam said.

"I will make you something twenty-two times better," I said. "My new recipe."

I hopped on the counter.

Julia put her hands in the air. "Guppeas."

"We'll play groceries in a minute, Jules," I said.

Julia shook her head no.

"*Guppeas* means 'pick me up, please,'" Sam said.

"The no means she doesn't want to play groceries. Thanks to you, she wants to stand on the counter."

I grabbed the ingredients and jumped down.

"Peanut butter is your new recipe?" Sam said. "I pass."

I curved my hand and went in for a scoop.

"You're going to eat a handful of peanut butter?" Sam asked. "What about your mom?"

"She likes me to eat protein," I said.

"You probably have a hundred colonies of germs on each finger," he said.

"Too late now," I said. "If she comes in I'll shove my hand in my pocket. But first, I'm shoving it in this box."

When I pulled it out it was covered with Fruit Loops.

"Usually I stick on chocolate chips, raisins, and mini-marshmallows," I said. "The more toppings, the better."

"I'm making that when I get home," Sam said. "But I'm using a spoon."

"Spoons are for the weak," I said.

"I wonder where Julia found my gum," Sam said.

That made Julia remember. She patted her head with both hands.

"Julia," Sam said. "Don't touch. The more hair in the gum, the bigger your bald spot will be. The bigger the bald spot, the more upset Mom will be."

Julia kept stirring her hair around.

"She's making it worse," I said.

"What if my mom blames me?" Sam said. "It'll be the death of OZ. Goodbye, Follies."

"Julia," I said. "Please stop. The nest is growing."

"Gooum," Julia said.

I gave her a blueberry bagel.

"Nogul," Julia said.

Julia pulled her own hair so hard she yipped.

"Why does gum have to stick to everything?" Sam said.

"Incoming idea!" I said. "Stop the stickiness, you'll stop the spread."

"Pizza!" Sam said.

"Bad idea!" I said.

"My dad's pizza dough starts off sticky," Sam said. "He adds flour until it stops sticking to the rolling pin."

"BOB-o-rama!" I said.

"Hold Julia's gum clump straight up in the air so it doesn't get worse," Sam said. "I'll get the flour from the pantry."

I used my clean hand so I could keep licking the Fruit Loops off my peanut-buttery hand.

Julia hissed air out of her nose like a mad horse.

"Julia, if I don't keep your gummy hair away from your ungummy hair, it will turn into such a big hairball that people will think you have a cat on your head," I told her.

"Ma-yow," Julia said.

She flopped into crawling position. I recaptured her hair. She went after my peanut butter hand.

"If you make me trade hands you'll have greasy, gummy hair," I said. "Do you want that?"

She jerked her head so hard she made me pull her hair and made herself cry.

"Julia, when you bobble your head it pulls your

hair," I repeated. "Sit still. I'll rub the spot to stop the sting."

That needed two hands. One to hold the gum hair. One to rub the sting. By the time the hurt stopped she had a head full of peanut butter.

She sat for a minute. Then she held out her hand and said, "Gooominny!"

"I don't have any gum," I told her. "You have it. In your hair."

"Goo-um," she said like she was in charge.

She reached out and pulled my lips open. "Gooomin?"

I stuck out my tongue. "No gum. All gone. Hurry up, Sam."

I could hear my parents and Mr. Alswang talking about the trip to Baltimore.

"Is buckwheat flour the same as regular flour?" Sam whispered loudly.

"I don't know," I said. "Look at it."

I could see Julia's lip was doing the pre-cry shake.

"Minbludda," she said.

I wiped her bagel on my pants and gave it to her.

Julia rolled it. "Gummm," she said. "Meegumm."

Sam came back.

"That took a week," I said.

"It was on the top shelf. I had to pile cookbooks on the stepstool, balance myself, and flip the bag over the edge with the mop handle."

"Take over holding Julia's head," I said. "She got a load of hair in my peanut butter."

"Open the buckwheat bag," Sam said. "The parents will be done talking any minute."

I pulled up the triangle on the top of the bag.

"Where's the gum?" Sam asked.

"Where you left it," I told him. "In her hair."

"Peanut butter and tangles are in her hair," Sam said. "But no gum."

Julia held out both hands. "Goom."

"You've got the wrong wad of hair," I said.

"Find the right wad," he said.

I kneeled next to Julia and sorted through her hair. "It was right there," I said.

"Did you pull it out by mistake?" Sam asked.

"That wouldn't be a mistake," I said. "But I didn't."

"Her hair feels disgusting," Sam said. "Greasy and gunky but not sticky."

"Ickeeee," Julia said.

"So icky I'm washing my hands," I said.

I used dish soap and Comet.

"You had peanut butter on your hands," Sam said. "You got it in Julia's hair."

"You're the one who told me to hold on to the gum patch," I said.

"I'm not blaming you," he said. "I think peanut butter disintegrated the gum."

"Is that possible?" I asked.

Sam's dad came through the swinging door and swooped up Baby Julia.

"How's my gummy girl?" Mr. Alswang asked.

"Gum," Julia said.

"What?" Mr. Alswang asked.

"GUM!" Julia yelled.

"Julia! I believe that's your first real word," Mr. Alswang said.

"Gum," Julia said again.

"I was hoping word one would be *Daddy*," he said. "But *gum* is a fine word too."

"GUM!" she said.

"Julia's impressed with gum," I said.

"But there's no more gum in her hair," Sam said.

"You cut out the gum?" Mr. Alswang said.

"I thought you and Mom would be mad if I did that," Sam said.

"You were right," Mr. Alswang said.

"We invented gum remover," Sam said.

"Peanut butter," I told him.

"George Washington Carver invented peanut butter," Mr. Alswang said.

"We're the ones who figured out that it gets gum out of hair," I said.

"That's the most useful discovery since baby gates," Mr. Alswang said.

He put Julia on his shoulders and carried her to the front hall.

"Julia said her first word," Mr. Alswang told my parents.

"It's *gum*," Sam said.

"Gum!" Julia yelled.

"Bravo!" my dad said.

"Hurrah!" Sam said.

"Who's the smartest wittle girl in the whole wide world?" my mom asked. She talks to babies like she's a baby. She thinks it fools them.

"GUM!" Julia said.

"Jules rules!" Sam yelled.

"We'd better get home so Mom can hear Julia's big news," Mr. Alswang said.

"Remember to come early tomorrow, Melonhead," Sam said.

"We have a project," I told my mom.

When I was in bed, my dad came in to say goodnight.

"I'm going to carry a peanut butter snack pack wherever I go," he said. "You never know when there will be a gum emergency."

That made me feel good.

"Congressman Buddy Boyd could get Dentyne stuck in his hair," I said.

"We'd have it out in a jiffy," my dad said.

"It wouldn't show," I said. "His hair is already greasy."

"The Congressman uses a lot of hair care products," my dad said.

"To look young?"

"That's what he believes," my dad answered. "Do you think it works?"

"Not at all," I answered.

"Me either," my dad said.

I went to sleep thinking that even though the dent was bad, one new business plus two discoveries still equals one good weekend.

21

UP TO OUR NECKS IN MONEY

I got up before my dad dragged me out of bed by my ankles. That's a sacrifice. I like being dragged.

First I checked messages.

Dear We-Fix-It Company,

Thanks for the fast reply. We'd be delighted to come home to a nicely pruned yard! Our house is 228 A Street SE. It's the one with a contemporary fence. Please send a bill. We'll pay you upon our return.

Thank you,
Hilary B.

I put on yesterday's cargo shorts and the official Cape May Point, NJ, Lifeguard shirt that Madam and Pop gave me for my birthday. It came from their vacation.

I was the last person to get to the kitchen. My dad was wearing a suit and a tie that used to be rejected. My mom was wearing sleeping shorts and her Moms On The Hill T-shirt.

"Good morning, M.O.T.H.," I said. "Good morning, Dad."

"Good morning, DB."

"Good morning, Sport."

I stuffed most of my cargo pockets with Joe's O's but I put Golden Grahams in the big pocket on my right leg. There was still a load of peanut butter stuck to the inside. By the time I got to school I'd have peanut butter–flavored Golden Grahams. If you don't think that's the flavor of the year, try it.

"I'll eat my bagel on the way to Sam's," I said.

"This is a kitchen, not a food court," my mom said. That is one of her favorite old sayings.

"Remember, our project is due today," I said. That wasn't a lie. Gluing shoes is a project and we told Pop we'd bring it to him today. "You said I should get things done on time."

"That is one of the Guidelines for Life," my dad said.

"So is Think of Others," I said. "By others I mean Jonique. If she makes it to June with no tardy marks, she'll get a medal on moving-up day. And if I'm late to Sam's, we'll be late for the footpool. That could throw her off."

My mom gets enthusiastic about prizes.

"There's an award for that?" she asked.

I nodded.

"You could win too, DB. You've been on time every day this year. That's almost a month."

"The medal is for never being late from kindergarten through fifth grade," I said. "Nobody has won since 1987."

"Jonique McBee has been on time every single day for six years?"

"So far," I said.

"That is a huge accomplishment," my mom said.

"It's not like Jonique is Ruth Wakefield or Clarence Birdseye," I said.

Being an inventor, I know about inventors. My mom only knows the usual ones plus two: 1. Ruth Wakefield, inventor of chocolate chip cookies; 2. Clarence Birdseye, inventor of frozen food. My mom says it would be a sad world if they hadn't gotten here before she did.

"Follow Jonique's example," my mom said. "One perfect year will still be an achievement."

"Here's a bagel with cream cheese and strawberry jam to go," my dad said. "And your water bottle."

"Chew every bite twenty times," my mom said. "You don't want to be one of those people who choke on bagels."

"I never heard of those people," I said.

"Probably because they choked," she said.

"Backpack packed?" my dad asked.

"I'll bet you can't say that three times fast," I said. He couldn't.

I found my homework and a geode I like to carry around and stuffed them in my backpack. My mom took advantage of my stillness and raked my hair with her fingernails.

My dad ruffled up my raked hair.

I grabbed my skateboard.

"I'm on the move, parents."

"Buckle your helmet," my dad said. "We want to protect that interesting brain of yours."

22

GLOOZE

The semi-second I swung open Sam's gate, he swung open the front door.

"The glue's in the basement," he said.

We climbed over the baby gate and clomped down the creaky steps to the Alswangs' spooky basement. The only basement with more tools is Pop's.

"Your mom didn't ask why we brought home someone else's shoes?" I asked.

"Why would she?" Sam asked.

"My mom would," I said.

"Your mom wouldn't see them because she makes people leave their shoes in the vestibule," Sam said.

"True," I said.

Julia screamed from the top of the steps, "Ewego, mego!"

"The basement is dangerous for babies," Sam yelled.

"GUM!" Julia yelled.

Her hands were curled around the top of the gate.

"She looks like she's in baby jail," I told Sam.

"She sort of is," he said.

I ran back up and handed her a scoop of Joe's O's from my cargo pocket.

"Gum," she said.

Mr. Alswang's glue collection is a world wonder.

"Plug in the hot glue gun, Son," I told Sam. "I'm a glue gun expert. I watched Mrs. McBee glue a pile of straw into a life-size scarecrow."

"Heat melts rubber," Sam said.

"You are right, McKnight," I said. "What's in the can that says Repair-a-Spare?"

"Glue and rubber patches. My mom bought it when my bike tire went flat."

"I wish we had a flat tire so we could try it out," I said.

I read the back of the Super-Strong pack. "'The strongest adhesive in the world! Repairs china, wood, rubber, and metal. Lasts and lasts! Dries in seconds! Dishwasher safe! Just pennies per use!' Who would put glue in the dishwasher?" I asked.

"Somebody who doesn't think about consequences," Sam said.

"That's not us," I said.

A baby rain boot bounced down the steps.

"Meee-me-mememe-me!" Julia screamed.

"There's only enough Super-Strong to do one sneaker," I said.

"Take it," Sam said. "I'll use Gorilla Glue on mine."

"Is it strong?" I asked.

"My mom used it to put my bed frame back together after the big collapse," he said.

"When we were playing Flying Leap?"

"No," he said. "When we were playing Storm the Castle."

"That was the greatest collapse."

Sam tried to open the Gorilla Glue.

"It's stuck like glue," he said.

"Because it is stuck with glue," I said. "Twist the top with pliers. But to avoid a snafu, Think Before Acting. We should wear goggles."

"Right you are, Candy Bar," Sam said. "I'll read your directions: 'Before applying, surfaces must be clean and dry.'"

"Check."

"'Spread glue evenly on both sides.'"

I did that.

"'Press parts together,'" Sam read. "'Wait five minutes before moving.'"

"That's a long time to stand still," I said.

"Don't think about moving," Sam said.

Once he said that, moving was the only thing I could think about.

"Oh, great," Sam said. "The Gorilla Glue instructions have been dripped on."

"Glue is like shampoo," I told him. "The directions don't change."

"Red alert!" Sam said. "The toe of your shoe has glue ooze!"

"Bet you can't say 'glue ooze' three times fast!" I said.

"Gloo ooze, clewz, glooze," Sam said.

"Told you," I said.

"Seriously," Sam said. "Look! Glooze is escaping."

"Throw me a rag," I said.

"No time. Just pinch it shut!" Sam said.

I grabbed the toe.

"Point the toe at the ceiling," Sam said.

"That will reverse the leak."

"Press the flap together," Sam said.

"I did, Kid."

Sam crossed his eyes at me.

He pulled back the flap and made a glue outline around the edge.

"Fill it in with a puddle of glue," I said. "Slap them together."

Baby Julia yelled down the steps. "Guh-hum!"

"No gum, Julia!" Sam yelled.

"One shoe, good as new," I said. "Walk and wear."

"Put it down," Sam said.

"I'm trying."

"Funny, Sonny."

"Not to me," I said.

"Are you seriously glued to Pop's shoe?"

I straightened my arm. The shoe dangled in midair.

"Actually," I admitted, "it's hilarious."

23

A STICKY SITUATION

"Gahum!" Julia whined.

"Julia!" Sam said. "Melonhead cannot drop what he's doing to bring you gum. Literally. He can't."

"Grab and yank," I told Sam.

I had to bite the insides of my cheeks to keep from making pig squeals. "You're peeling skin off my finger bones."

"If your skin had peeled, you'd be free," Sam said.

Mrs. Alswang yelled down the stairs. "You have two minutes to get to Jimmy T's. The Footpool's waiting."

"Can you please throw down our backpacks,

Mom?" Sam hollered. "We're leaving through the basement door."

"Meet me at the top of the steps!" Mrs. Alswang yelled.

"Coming, Mom!" he yelled.

He gave Pop's sneaker a sharp pull.

"Quit it," I whispered. "You're making my fingers feel like porcupines rolling on pointed rocks."

He ran up and got the backpacks. On the way back he grabbed a bag off Mrs. Alswang's wrapping paper shelf.

"Shove the shoe in the bag and loop the handle around your thumb," he said.

"Is there a bag that's not covered with hearts and sparkles?"

"The other one has baby rattles," Sam said.

"I'll take rattles," I said.

Sam grabbed it and swooped down and scooped up Pop's shoe.

"Gotta fly, Guy!" he said.

It's hard to put on your backpack with one arm. "Give me a hand, Rubber Band."

"Race me, Flea!"

Sam got to the crosswalk before I even got past the dreaded Mrs. Lee's house. She is a tattler who calls people's mothers. Especially ours. We try to keep out of her sight.

"Wait up!" I yelled.

When we got to Jimmy T's, Jonique and Lucy Rose had their hands on their hips. Lucy Rose was tapping her cowgirl boot on the bricks.

"Have you ever heard of time management?" Jonique said.

"If Jonique gets a tardy because of you two, I will be mad at both of you until I'm in my thirties," Lucy Rose said.

"Let's rock and roll," Pip said. She took off so fast everybody had to catch up.

"Who's the baby present for?" Jonique asked.

"If I show you, you'll tell the entire school."

"We wouldn't," Lucy Rose said. "Nobody cares about presents that are for a baby."

"Is it embarrassing?" Pip asked.

"Melonhead doesn't get embarrassed," Jonique said.

Sometimes I do, but I don't tell them.

I let go of the bag. The shoe hung from my fingers.

It was like I gave those girls a five-pound sack of Pixy Stix.

"How did you get stuck to a shoe?" Jonique asked.

"By mistake," I said.

"Is that Pop's sneaker?" Lucy Rose asked.

"Don't make a humongous deal out of it," I said.

"On the good side, Pop's sneaker is fixed for life," Sam said.

"On the bad side, Melonhead will have to crawl next to Pop wherever he goes," Jonique said.

Lucy Rose picked up my arm and looked at all sides of the problem.

"Do you know your three biggest fingers are stuck to your thumb?" she asked.

"Also each other," I said.

"Like the Fantastico pizza chef!" Pip said.

"The skinny-mustache guy," Sam said. "The one who kisses his fingertips and says 'Fantastico!'"

Pip did an imitation.

"If I kiss my fingers, Pop's shoe will kick me in my face," I said.

"Cut it off," Jonique said.

"My finger?" I asked.

"The shoe," Pip said.

"Are you nuts?" Sam said. "Melonhead could get cut."

"I'd live," I said.

"Sure, but if you bleed all over Pop's shoe we'll have to return his seven bucks," Sam said.

Jonique interrupted. "OZ is now OO."

"What?" Pip said.

"Operation Zero situations is now Operation One situation," Lucy Rose said.

"OZ is still OZ," I said. "This is a freak workplace accident. Completely different."

"Check out the Safety in the Workplace poster in Mr. Johnson's custodian's closet," Sam said.

"What's it say?" Pip asked.

"Wear eye goggles because you can't predict when a freak accident is going to happen," I said. "That's why they're freak."

"A glued shoe is a situation," Lucy Rose said.

"We reject that," Sam said. "And stop saying 'situation,' because we are not missing out on Follies Park."

"Melonhead!" Jonique said. "Focus! You can't walk into school with a shoe on your hand."

"Why not?" Sam said.

"The number one reason has blond hair and wears skorts that match her hair bands," Pip said.

Ashley's in our class. She lives to get me sent to Mr. Pitt's office. Mr. Pitt is like the Reflection Table only infinity times more boring. His top sentence is "Let's talk about why you made this choice."

Lucy Rose looked at me with dog eyes. "We will save you from utter humiliation and disgrace, Melonhead."

That's the Law of Footpool. If you are stuck or if a shoe is stuck to you, the F-pool will try to save you. Even if the snafu was caused by your own knuckleheadedness. That's because we have Character, Loyalty, and Courage. Pop says if you don't have CLC, it doesn't matter what you do have. Even if you're a millionaire baseball player who never loses and owns a private island and a fleet of dolphins. I agree with Pop, except owning dolphins could make up for some stuff.

"We need a BOB," Sam said.

24
CRASH LANDING

Kids were running around the playground. Parents were standing. Mr. Pitt was wandering, looking for rule breakers.

"Four minutes until first bell," I said. "Dump my backpack on the mulch in case something useful is in it."

Here's what we found, not counting homework, lunch, and my geode: 1. One mini Purell hand sanitizer on a key chain. 2. A small backup sanitizer with no key chain. 3. Neosporin. 4. Chopsticks. 5. Two quarters and one nickel. My mom put in everything except the chopsticks.

"There's the warning bell," Lucy Rose said. "I am sorry to say it, but you are D-Double Doomed."

"Melonhead, does it hurt to swing your arm?" Jonique asked.

"Like a shark bite," I said.

"Too bad," Jonique said. "Do it. Swinging might weaken the shoe glue."

"I don't mind a shark bite," I said. "I do mind the whole school watching. Surround me."

Pip and Sam took one side and Lucy Rose and Jonique walked on the other. I felt like I was the real T-POTUS surrounded by the Secret Service.

"Swing," Sam said.

I did. Lots of times. Halfway across the soccer field I yowled. "This hurts more than when I got my elbow stuck in the bleacher," I said.

"There's no blood," Pip said. "Keep swinging."

I swung eighteen times.

The miracle came on the nineteenth try. Pop's sneaker broke off and soared like Spider-Man.

Who knows how far it would have gone if it hadn't hit Mr. Pitt's stomach.

Question: There were over three hundred kids on the playground. How did Mr. Pitt know I was the one who launched the shoe?

He zeroed in on me in a New York second.

"I'm sorry. It was an accident, Mr. Pitt."

"A freak accident," Lucy Rose added.

"Hurling a shoe is not an accident," Mr. Pitt said.

"I wanted to hurl it," I said. "I didn't mean for it to kick your guts."

"Report to my office," Mr. Pitt said.

It's not so easy to carry a backpack when your fingers are stuck together.

25

IN THE MIDDLE OF TROUBLE

This was my first time in Mr. Pitt's office since the last week of fourth grade.

"You changed your office," I said. "And you got a peace poster."

"The school board says children respond to bean bag chairs and soft lighting," Mr. Pitt said.

"I don't think I'm responding," I said.

"Pull up a bean bag, Mr. Melon."

I picked the one that looked like a baseball.

Mr. Pitt sat across from me. I do not think he enjoys sitting on a giant bean bag.

He dropped Pop's shoe on the floor in between us.

"Can you explain why you thought it was appropriate to throw a shoe?" Mr. Pitt asked.

"I didn't think it was appropriate at all," I said.

Mr. Pitt leaned forward.

"I'm glad you see that," Mr. Pitt said. "Now tell me why you did it."

"I had no control," I said.

"Thank you for admitting that," he said. "Lack of self-control is a problem for many kids your age."

"I meant I had no shoe control," I said. "Also I didn't throw it."

"Adam," Mr. Pitt said in a testy way. "It's important that we have an honest dialogue."

"I swung it," I said.

Mr. Pitt looked annoyed.

"I'm sorry it kicked you in your guts," I said.

"Tell me, what motivated this hostility?"

What does that mean?

"Isn't motivated a good thing?" I asked.

"I am asking what made you throw a sneaker on a crowded playground."

"I wanted to get rid of it," I said.

"I'm sure you could find a better way to dispose of a shoe," Mr. Pitt said.

"If *dispose* means 'throw away,' we can't. It's not my shoe."

"After state testing is over we'll invite your parents in to discuss why throwing things at people strikes you as hilarious," Mr. Pitt said.

"Could you just invite my dad?" I asked. "Those kinds of meetings upset my mom. The next thing you know she'll be speed-breathing from worry."

"Remember that the next time you want to chuck a shoe," he said. "Now go join your class."

26
THE VERY LONG DAY

I thought Ms. Mad was going to ask why I had my hand in my pocket. But all she said was, "You're just in time for multiplication warm-ups."

All we do these days is warm up. Starting tomorrow we have state testing, even though Washington, D.C., is not a state. Where's the fairness in that?

"Pick up your number two pencils," Ms. Mad said. "And begin."

I became an instant lefty.

After Time's Up, Ms. Mad looked at my worksheet.

"Did a two-toed chicken write this for you?" she asked.

"No," I said.

"Tidiness is important," she said. "The tests are not graded by humans."

A picture of gorillas with red pencils popped into my head. I'd like to see that in real life.

You would be bothered to know all the things you can't do when you're forced to keep one hand under your desk. Lean back in your chair, for one thing. Or tap your pencil for another. When my ear itched I had to reach across my face to scratch it.

Every day at ten o'clock we have to stop for Words to the Wise. They echo because of the PA system. Today's announcer was Mr. Pitt.

"Today's topic is Lunchroom Safety Begins with You," Mr. Pitt said. "It is every student's responsibility to use the trash cans provided. Leaving food and lunch bags on the tables makes more work for Mr. Johnson. And it can put others at risk. Yesterday, I slipped on a piece of abandoned bologna."

All the kids in our class had a fit of uncontrollable laughing. Ms. Mad turned away from us. I couldn't see her face, but her shoulders jiggled so much I suspected her. I mean of laughing, not of abandoning bologna.

"I could have been gravely injured," Mr. Pitt said.

"I doubt anybody could die from slipping on bologna," I whispered to Lucy Rose.

"*Gravely* means 'seriously,'" Lucy Rose whispered. "It doesn't have to do with actual graves."

Mr. Pitt read a list called Risky Foods That, When Left on the Floor, Are a Danger to Others. Jell-O is one of them.

The second he was done Ms. Mad said, "Who's got Dance Fever?"

Then she played a song and everybody did fast crazy dances for sixty seconds.

We usually have Dance Fever after Words to the Wise. W to the W makes people fidgety. Dance Fever also helps us practice looking lively when we do our show, *This Week in Washington, D.C.*

We take turns having news jobs. Ms. Mad records it. On Fridays we edit it for the archive. Then kids of the future will be able to see what life was like in our time.

"Hayes Anderson, come up and announce the Headline of the Week, please," Ms. Mad said.

"Mayor Promises New Community Center to Adams Morgan," Hayes said.

Hannah was this week's Opinion Maker.

"My opinion is that a community center should be for the entire community. Nobody should get their own."

"Adams Morgan is a neighborhood, not a person," Ashley said.

"Hannah is from England," Kathleen said. "You can't expect her to know that."

"I agree," Hannah said.

Nicholas Levy reported on sports. "The Oyster-Adams Tigers beat the Murch Mustangs," he said. "But if Maret beats the Tigers on Friday, it's All Hail the Frogs!"

Nicholas sounds like a real sports announcer. He stretches words. It's like he has extra air in his chest.

Then Ms. Mad said, "Next up is Adam Melon, with the WOW! report."

"Can somebody else do it?" I asked.

"I will!" the whole class shouted.

"It's your turn," Ms. Mad said. "Here's your microphone."

I took it with my left hand.

Cole was doing the Countdown to Air, but Ms. Mad stopped him before he got to one.

"Adam, take your hand out of your armpit and relax," she said.

I stuffed my glued hand in my front pocket.

"Is there a problem?" Ms. Mad asked.

I was about to fake a stomachache when I was struck by a BOB.

"Hell-ooo, Wah-shing-ton, Deeee Cee!" I said. "This is Melonhead Melon, coming to you live with the WOW! report. This week's temperature was in the high nineties. The air felt like glue."

The footpool laughed when I said "glue."

"Luckily, on Friday afternoon a car hit the fire hydrant in front of the Library of Congress. The water shot up to around fifty feet. It also squirted out both sides. People ran around in it. Even adults. The second lucky thing was that it took the water company over six hours to shut off the valve."

I pulled my hand out of my pocket and swooshed it through the air.

"Here is my rating for that day."

I kissed the tops of my fingers and yelled, "Fantastico!"

Some people clapped for me.

At dismissal Ms. Mad said I should stay after.

I automatically sat down at the Reflecting Table.

"Come here and show me your hand," Ms. Mad said.

I put my right hand out.

"The other one."

She examined it.

"Why are your fingers stuck together?" she asked.

I explained about Pop's shoe and how I got it detached.

"How's the sneaker?" she asked.

"Fixed," I said.

"All right, then," Ms. Mad said.

"Not all right," I said. "It crash-landed into Mr. Pitt's stomach. Now he won't give it back."

"Sometimes you really are a Melonhead," she said.

"Thanks," I said. "But I feel like a nut."

"Get to Nurse Fanny's office before she leaves for the day," Ms. Mad said.

"She'll just do what she always does," I said. "Take my temperature and put Neosporin on it."

"I hope she has a better idea than that," Ms. Mad said.

Nurse Fanny was packing up when I got to her office.

"What is it this time?" she asked.

I showed her.

Guess what she did?

She squirted Neosporin on my fingers.

I'm not kidding.

"Can I go show this to Ms. Mad?" I asked.

"No," she said. "Rub the Neosporin into the glue."

I bet she's not even a real nurse.

"Keep rubbing," she said.

She's definitely a total fake. No wonder she only has two cures.

"I'm okay now," I said. "Thanks for the ointment. I'll see you another day."

"Keep rubbing," she said.

Ater a while she helped rub my glued skin.

"Try separating your fingers," she said.

"Hey! My thumb's semi-free," I said.

She squirted on another squiggle.

"Who knew Neosporin would work?" I asked.

"I did," Nurse Fanny said. "I'm a professional."

It was like she read my mind.

"Why does it work?" I asked.

"Petroleum breaks down superglue. Petroleum jelly is in Neosporin. Fingernail polish remover works faster, but your skin is torn up. It would sting like a hornet."

"You are a real nurse!" I said. "I mean, a great, excellent, finger-freeing genius of a nurse. Thank you."

I ran back to show Not-So-Bad Ms. Mad.

"Amazing," she said.

Then Ms. Mad amazed me.

"How did you get Pop's shoe back?" I asked.

"I told Mr. Pitt you weren't aiming for him," she said. "He said he would've returned the sneaker if you had explained the situation."

"It wasn't a situation," I said. "More of a snafu."

"Stay away from superglue," she said. "At least until after state testing."

27

EASY MONEY

"Let's go, Joe," I said. "We've got bushes to cut and shoes to deliver."

"Adult Fix-It men have it E-Z," Sam said. "All they do is work. We also have to work and go to fifth grade."

"Plus, they can drive," I said. "And they don't have to borrow tools."

It was easy to find the Bensons' house.

"I would not call this fence temporary," Sam said.

"Wood is temporary compared to iron," I told him.

"Mrs. Benson was right," Sam said. "Her yard is a wreck."

"A fun wreck," I said.

"Most wrecks are," Sam said.

"You know what looks rich?" I asked. "Bushes that are cut into twirls."

"Yes!" Sam agreed.

I bowed like I was a judo expert and yelled, "Thank you, Yard Crew!"

"You carve that bush. I'll do the one on the other side of the walkway," Sam said.

"Hold on. We should think of OZ and ask ourselves: Do we know how to carve twirls?"

"Twirls are E-Z P-Z," Sam said.

"I agree, McGee."

"Race you!" Sam said.

"When we step back to look at the big picture we are going to shout 'Magnificent!'" I said.

We did. "It's odd how the edges look smooth when you're cutting and hacked when you're done," Sam said.

"Sam," I said. "I can describe these bushes in two words: *abstract design*. Remember what Ms. Mad said on the Hirshhorn Museum field trip?"

"'Art does not have to be a certain way,'" Sam said.

"And these bushes are not a certain way. These bushes look like they were carved by famous abstract bush designers," I said.

"That stuff growing over the basement windows must be the Swedish ivy," Sam said. "Ready to pull it down?"

"I'm on the case."

I was pretending I was harvesting a spaghetti tree when a bird's nest fell on my head.

"Lucky break. No eggs!" I yelled.

"What's next? Weeds or trees?" Sam asked.

"Weeds for me," I said. "Trees for you."

"How do we know if it's a weed?" Sam asked.

"If it doesn't have a flower, it's a weed," I said.

Finally we were done.

"Mrs. Benson is going to tell her friends to hire the We-Fix-It Company!"

"Did we cut the crape myrtles?" Sam asked.

"We cut everything," I said. "Some of them must have been myrtles."

We filled three trash cans and wheeled them out to the curb for pickup. We would have had more trash but we kept some souvenirs of nature. The best one is a perfect Y-stick. I'm going to turn it into a slingshot.

"Next stop is my house," Sam said. "We'll grab Pop's other shoe and deliver them."

"Pop is going to say we're geniuses," I said. "And time managers."

"He'll be right."

28

THE SURPRISE WE DIDN'T WANT

Julia heard us coming and screamed "GUM!" at the top of her baby lungs.

"She is getting demanding," Sam said.

"Wow," Sam's mom said. "What did you do to get so dirty?"

"Fixed up the Bensons' yard," Sam said. "She's going to pay us."

"Just in time," Sam's mom said.

"Why?" Sam asked.

"Daddy told me about the teapot disaster," she said.

Julia was pulling on the bottom of my shorts.

"Can you tell me why you thought it was a swell idea to throw pizza sauce?" Mrs. Alswang said.

"It's because we're boys," I said. "It's how we think."

"Weestink," Julia said.

I hooted. Sam acted like a pterodactyl smelling its wingpits.

"*Stink* is not a nice word, Julia," Mrs. Alswang said.

Julia waved her finger at her mom.

"Ewes tink."

We laughed like baboons.

"Leftovers are in the fridge," Mrs. Alswang said. "Make yourselves meatball subs."

Make-it-yourself is one of the top things about Sam's house.

When we were stuffed, Sam said, "Melonhead, wipe off the counter. I'll get the shoe."

Sam's shriek from the basement was so loud that Julia started wailing.

Mrs. Alswang jumped over the baby gate, yelling, "I'm coming!"

"Me too," I said. "Help is on the way!"

I do not know how to explain what went on in the basement while we were at school.

"How did this go so wrong?" Sam asked.

"I don't know," Mrs. Alswang said. "I'm glad you're not hurt. Your scream scared me."

"Mama!" Julia screamed.

"She said *Mama*!" Mrs. Alswang yelled. "*Mama*'s her second word! Mama's coming, baby girl!"

"Remember when we helped Pop mulch the far backyard?" I asked Sam.

He nodded.

"And the next day the mulch was spotted with yellow piles that looked like dog throw-up?"

"And Pop said there's a fungus a-mung-us."

Sam shook me by my shoulders and screamed, "How did fungus get in Pop's shoe?"

"I'm not saying it is fungus," I said. "I'm saying it looks like fungus."

"It's like somebody stuffed a big triangle of foaming, dripping, rock-hard stink cheese in between the bottom of the sneaker and the rubber flap!" Sam shouted.

"Disgusting, unbendable cheese that turned Pop's shoe into a high-heeled sneaker," I said. "Only in reverse, since the front of the shoe is two inches higher than the back."

We felt so bad that we were going to disappoint Pop that we decided to wait until after Baltimore to tell him.

29
BALTIMORE

The first thing about Baltimore Metal Crafters is that when you go, you will wish you lived there.

It's a short building that's half underground. There are no signs, just a number. At first I thought it was an FBI hideout.

When my dad pulled open the metal door, all I could say was "Take a nose full of this!"

"It's the third-worst smell I ever sniffed," Sam said.

"I don't usually rate bad smells," my dad said. "But this is a doozy."

"Dad, here's how you can tell it's the third worst," I said. "Even after you have been standing in it for a while, it still stinks just as bad."

"Thanks for bringing me, Mr. Melon," Sam said.

"You're welcome, Sam," my dad said.

We passed the first door. "Smells like there's a plastic fabricator in there," my dad said.

"How do you know?" I asked.

"I hear the exhaust vents," he said. "And hot plastic is a smell that lingers."

"Do you think we'd smell more if we had trimmed our nose hairs, Dad?" I asked.

"Don't tell me you've been trimming your nose hairs," my dad said.

"We haven't," I said. "But once we pay for the dent and buy Mom a Jet Ski we're planning to buy a nose hair trimming machine at Grubb's. It is extremely interesting."

"We've been looking for one in Senator Lavin's trash," Sam said. "No luck."

"Nose hair trimmers aren't things people throw away," I said.

When we opened the last door I could have fainted. Not from the smell, which was not at all disappointing.

"We're in Ali Baba's cave," I said.

"There are things here I never saw in my life," Sam said.

One was a big clear box with armholes. A man was standing in front of the box with his hands inside. If he wanted, he could have clapped.

"That's a spray booth," my dad said. "It keeps the chemicals out of his lungs. And if he sprayed out here, dust would stick to the finish."

"When I knocked over my mom's nail polish on the back porch, pollen stuck to it," Sam said. "It's still like that."

"You didn't clean it up?" my dad asked.

"I thought it would evaporate," Sam said.

"Are you Mr. Phillips?" I yelled.

"I'm Roland Phillips," he said.

"Want some help?" I asked

"Lacquering's a one-man job, and it takes the time it takes," he said. "Sit tight and I'll get to you. Look around."

"Is that a propane tank?" I asked.

"It's an antique samovar," my dad said.

Sam made a muscle pose. "Invented by a man named Sam."

"What does it do?" I asked.

"It boils water," my dad explained. "When you pull down the carved ring, hot water comes out of the spout."

"You mean snout," Sam said.

"Only if the samovar is shaped like a pig," my dad said. "Otherwise it's a spout.

"No one ever told me it was *spout*," I said.

"Compared to the samovar, T-POTUS is barely three percent cool," Sam said.

"But can a samovar lead our country?" my dad asked.

"Not T-POTUS the president," I said. "T-POTUS the teapot. The actual POTUS beats a samovar."

A lady came in and picked up a bucket of black forks.

She looked at T-POTUS.

"Not the worst dent we've seen today," she said.

"Wait until Mom hears that," I said.

"Can we take the tour of this place?" Sam asked.

She laughed. "No one has ever asked for a tour."

"You are making that up," I said.

"I'm Cheyenne. Do you want to see Before and Afters?"

"Absolutely," my dad said.

"This brass light fixture used to look like that one," Cheyenne said.

"Why?" I asked.

"You'd be dirty too if you hàdn't had a bath in fifty years," she said. "They're from the Baltimore Basilica on Cathedral Street. They're here to get the Four Rs: Repaired, Replated, Restored, and Rewired."

"This is the best job in Baltimore, isn't it?" I said.

"I think it's the best job in the state of Maryland," Cheyenne said.

Sam pointed at a tall tube by the wall. "That's a torpedo, isn't it?" he asked.

Cheyenne laughed. "It's an old fire extinguisher," she said. "The owner wants to turn it into a lamp."

"Why?" I asked. "A lamp doesn't do anything but light up. A fire extinguisher can be turned into a weapon or a game. Also, it can put out fires."

"Our fire extinguisher is red," Sam said. "How come this one's metal?"

"They used to be made of copper," Cheyenne said. "Someone had painted this one yellow."

"Why?"

"Bad taste, I guess," Cheyenne said. "We dipped it and stripped it. Now we have to polish the copper so it will shine like it did in 1930."

"You should use Destructionator," Sam said. "Melonhead invented it."

"It's a speed cleaner," I said.

Mr. Phillips walked over from the spraying box.

"I'm ready to learn."

We told him how to make it.

"Destructionator is going to be a new formula here," he said. "I owe you one."

"Do you happen to have any hand sanitizer?" Cheyenne asked.

"I always have hand sanitizer," I said.

"Melonhead's mom hooked a squeeze bottle onto his backpack strap," Sam said. "He stuffed it inside so people can't see."

Supersonic brain-to-brain message to Sam: *Stop embarrassing me.*

"My wife is opposed to germs," my dad said.

"Let me show you a trick," Mr. Phillips said.

When he was done, Sam and I couldn't believe our eyeballs.

"But that only works on light tarnish," he said. "Now I'll teach you the professional secret."

He came back with a big orange box with a muscle arm on the front and a roll of tinfoil.

"I'll boil water, boss," Cheyenne said.

He showed us how the professionals make it. "Now," he said, "I'll put this candlestick in halfway so you can see the proof."

We waited a few minutes before he pulled it out.

"That's a miracle!" Sam said.

"That's science," Mr. Phillips said.

The only bad part of the day was when he told us the price of the dent removing.

"I thought that was how much it cost to go to college," I said.

"I wish it weren't so expensive," Mr. Phillips said. "But it takes time to get it right."

"Before I say yes, I need to talk to my wife," my dad said.

"You know this teapot isn't worth very much," Mr. Phillips said.

"We know," I told him.

"How do you de-dent it?" Sam asked.

"With a hammer," Mr. Phillips said.

"That's what I told Mom!" I said. "She wouldn't let me do it."

Since we were new customers, Mr. Phillips gave us a valuable hunk of deer antler for free. He keeps them around for when knife handles break.

30

THE UNSATISFIED CUSTOMER

My mom was waiting on the porch.

"What did they say?" she asked.

My dad told her the price.

"That's a lot of money," she said.

"Don't you worry," I told her. "We'll earn it."

We raced upstairs and checked for messages.

"More mail, Whale," Sam said.

I hit Open.

"More money, Sonny."

"Uh-oh," Sam said, after he read the note.

Dear We-Fix-It Company,

I gather you were unable to work on our yard while we were away. Perhaps rain prevented you from transforming our scrubby lot into a showplace. Please reschedule.

Mrs. H. Benson

"How can she say that?" I asked Sam. "Plants do not grow back in a day."

"What more can she expect two boys to do?" Sam said.

"Men," I said. "She expected men."

Dear Mrs. Benson,

Please explain what the matter is with your yard.

Sincerely,
The We-Fix-It Company

*****

Dear Sirs,

When can I expect delivery of the rustic birthday birdhouse?

G.W.

I smacked my own forehead.

"We forgot about the birdhouse."

"E-Z P-Z," Sam said. "We'll cut a door in a big plastic soda bottle. Birds can fly inside."

"It'll be rustic if we glue sticks on it," I said.

"I have glue anxiety," Sam said.

"Look," I said. "New message."

Welcome to Capitol Hill,
We-Fix-It Company!

Our home needs several repairs. None are major. Just things that happen when boys are in the house.

1. Regular punching has made our screen door look as if cannon balls have been bounced off the wire.

2. The backyard gate was used as a rock-transporting system. It now drags along the bricks in the alley.

3. Handprints can only be washed off so many times. The wall on the side of the staircase needs painting. Just the part opposite the railing. No need to paint the entire wall, as this will need to be done again in a few months.

    4. Tighten kitchen chair legs.

    5. Power wash black dots caused by Fourth of July snakes.

    If I may ask a favor, would you mind if two young boys watched you work? Please send me your rates so I can budget for repairs.

    Thanks very much.

"She should tell her kids to shape up," I said.

"It's probably from Bart Bigelow's mom," Sam said.

I typed our answer.

    Dear Sir or Lady,

    We'll fix your house and teach those boys. We are in favor of kids working. I have an ancestor who got a job when she was twelve and she had a happy life. Our professional opinion is that by the time your children are twelve, they should be able to do electricity. Please send your address so we can come over.

                    *****

We-Fix-It Company,

You ask what is the matter with my yard? The answer is: the same things that were the matter when I first contacted you. Only now it's even shaggier. If you don't want the job, please let me know.

Mrs. H. B.

*****

Dear Mrs. H. Benson,

We have heard that the customer is always right, but you are not. No offense. Your yard used to be a wreck. Now it's not. Your bill is $11.

From,
The T.W.F.I.C.
(The We-Fix-It Company)

P.S. Is this about the myrtles?

*****

Gentlemen,

Thank you. The boys will enjoy working with real professionals. By working, I mean watching. At eleven, they are not old enough to handle screwdrivers, hammers, nails, and other tools. (But I did laugh at your joke about electricity.) Can you come some afternoon this week? The boys have the afternoons off because of city-wide testing. I look forward to hearing from you.

"It will be weird if we know them," I said.

T.W.F.I.C.,

Why would I send you $11 for doing nothing?

H.B.

*****

Dear H.B.,

Do these pictures of rocks and a slingshot stick and a bird's nest look familiar? They came out of your yard. That's proof. You owe us $11. Please pay.

T.W.F.I.C.

"Let's not take any more unsatisfied customers," I said.

"At least this one gave me an idea," Sam said.

Dear Ma'am,

We will come paint your hall and fix your screen door tomorrow, but we need your address. Please send it.

Professionally yours,
The WFI Co.

"Another message!" Sam said.
I high-fived him. "We put the *pop* in popular."

Dear We-Fix-It,

Sorry! I signed off without giving you my address. Our address is 452 Fifth Street.

Thank you.

We were more shocked than Ben Franklin would have been if he actually did the kite, key, and lightning experiment.

31

THINGS GET WORSE

"Adam and Sam!" my mom screamed. "Come downstairs! This. Minute."

She was standing at the bottom of the steps with her arms folded in that mad way.

"You should have said you were my mother!" I said.

"I had no idea I was your mother," she said. "I mean, I had no idea you two were the We-Fix-It Company."

"How else would we pay for the teapot, Mrs. Melon?"

"Please tell me I am your only customer," my mom said.

"You're our only satisfied customer," Sam said.

"I am far from satisfied," she said. "I've seen We-Fix-It ads all over Capitol Hill. The M.O.T.H.s can't stop talking about the new handymen in the neighborhood! There's a sign in Grubb's drugstore! What were you thinking? Oh, no! Mrs. Benson said We-Fix-It was coming to landscape her yard."

"What is 'landscape,' exactly?" Sam asked.

"Making the yard look good," my mom said.

She was speed-breathing.

"We did," I said. "But Mrs. Benson says we didn't. She's a deadbeat no-payer."

"By the way, do you know what a crape myrtle looks like?" Sam asked.

My mom sat on the rickety chair by the hall table. It's supposed to be for decoration only.

"Who are your other unhappy customers?" she asked.

"Pop, but we haven't told him yet," I said.

"What happened?"

"His shoe expanded," Sam said.

"We'll get back to that," she said.

"George E. West is our other customer," I said. "He's not unsatisfied yet."

She made a small smile. "I'm happy to say I don't know George E. West."

"We don't either," I said. "He ordered a rustic birdhouse."

"You're working for strangers?"

"Businessmen can't just work for their friends, Mrs. Melon," Sam said.

"Honestly, Adam! Did you think about asking an adult?"

"I honestly did not."

"Sam?"

"Nope," Sam said.

"Put on a clean shirt, Adam," my mom said. "And lend one to Sam. In business it's respectful to look good when you have apologies to make."

"What apologies?" I asked.

"The three of us are walking over to Mr. West's house to cancel the birdhouse."

"He's depending on us," I said. "His wife's birthday is tomorrow."

"Plus, we have a solution," Sam said.

"Then we're going to Mrs. Benson's house to apologize for not trimming her yard," my mom said.

"We didn't trim," Sam said.

"We chopped, which is a load more work," I said.

"Then you'll return Pop's money and ask how much you owe him for his sneakers."

"That's not fair, Mom. Now we have to get all new customers."

"The We-Fix-It Company is out of business. I'm sorry."

32

GOING BROKE

"Can you wait on the sidewalk, Mom?" I said. "Businessmen do not bring their mothers with them."

"Okay," she said. I could tell she did not want to agree.

A lady with one shoe on and one shoe off opened the door.

"Sorry," she said. "I just got home from the emergency room."

"Is Mr. West here?" I said.

"Trader Joe's doesn't close until nine," she said.

"It takes him that long to buy food?" Sam asked.

"He works there," she said.

"Oh," Sam said. "Can you give him this bag?"

"Certainly," she said.

"It's fragile," Sam told her.

"See you later," I said. "We hope you feel better."

"Why?" she said.

"So you don't have to go back to the emergency room," I said.

She laughed. "I go every day. I'm a doctor."

"On to the Bensons'," my mom said.

We followed her for two blocks until, out of the pure blue, she stopped in front of a gray-and-white house.

"Cool fence," Sam said.

It looked like black squares.

"Quite contemporary for the neighborhood," my mom said.

"What does *contemporary* mean?" I asked.

"Not permanent," Sam said.

"Modern," my mom said.

"*Contemporary* means 'modern'?" I asked. "I doubt many people know that."

"It's not surprising Mrs. Benson is unhappy," my

mom said. "It doesn't look like you did a thing to this yard."

"Because it's not her yard," I said.

"Or their house," Sam told her.

"It certainly is," my mom said. "Mr. Melon and I have been here for dinner."

"Mom, the Bensons live on the other side of East Capitol Street," I said. "In Northeast."

She swung her head around.

"It's an easy mistake to make, Mrs. Melon," Sam said. "Tourists do it all the time."

My mom opened the gate, walked up the steps, and knocked on the front door.

I admit I was shocked when Mrs. Benson opened it.

"Betty! What a treat to see you. Come in. You too, boys."

Mrs. Benson thought the mistake was so hilarious that she gave us chocolate milk.

"That means you kids trimmed the Bruces' yard," Mrs. Benson said.

"Oh, no!" my mom said. "I take Jazzercise with Peggy Bruce. What must she have thought when she came home and saw her chopped-up yard?"

"She thought, Wow! Some great person came over and carved our bushes into shapes," I said.

"Shapes?" my mom said. "What kind of shapes?"

"The Bruces will never know," Mrs. Benson said. "They're in Metarie, Louisiana. They'll be there for another month at least. Their daughter, Rachel, had twins again."

"That's fantastic!" my mom said.

"Isn't it?" Mrs. Benson said. "Boys named Rivers and Robert. Peg is thrilled to bits."

"I mean fantastic, their yard will have regrown by the time they get home!" my mom said.

"That's the problem with yards," Mrs. Benson said.

"Of course, babies are nice too," my mom added.

33

PRESENTING THE CHEESE SHOE

"My mom doesn't jump over fences," I told Pop.

"Quite right. Madam is one of the few ladies who enjoy that."

"She does?" my mom asked.

My mom doesn't always get jokes.

"Come into the morning room," Madam said.

"The boys have something to give you," my mom said.

I wished she wouldn't use her funeral voice.

"We brought your shoes back," Sam told Pop.

I took them out of my backpack.

"Those are some shoes," Pop said. "I've never seen such a repair."

"We're sorry we let you down," I said.

"Let me down?" he said.

I pointed to the giant wedge of drippy, hard, cheesy foam.

"If you wear them, you'll feel like you're walking on a pogo stick."

"They're ruined," Sam said.

"Ruined?" Pop said. "You are boy geniuses! This shoe is all Madam needs to become a competitive fence jumper."

"Really?" Sam said. "I thought that was a joke."

"Sam," Pop said. "I hope you are not one of those people who make fun of fence jumping."

Sam didn't say anything.

"This shoe will give Madam a running start and the high front will propel her up and over," Pop said. "It will make up for her shortness of leg!"

"Are you joking?" Sam asked.

"Not about being happy with the job," Pop said. "It was a great experiment."

"That flopped," I said.

"Some experiments work. Some don't. The important thing is that you do them," Pop said. "But you already know that from your blow-up pants experiment."

"What blow-up pants experiment?" my mom asked.

"They were a thrill while they lasted," Pop said.

I got Pop's money out of my pocket and shook off the cereal dust.

"Here's your refund," I said.

"Hold on to it," Pop said. "Madam will need more deliveries. Her tea for young people was a great success. They ate the Divas' itty-bitty food and discussed classic books."

"I wish I'd been invited to teas like that when I was in college," my mom said. "I enjoy discussing the arts. What books are these young people reading?"

"*Hop on Pop* is popular," Madam said. "That may be because my husband lies on the floor and lets the guests hop over him."

"There was also a great deal of hopping *on* Pop," Pop said. "Sam's sister, Julia, was among the hop-ons."

"Oh," my mom said. "This was a tea party for very young people."

"Some were very," Pop said. "Others were three or four."

"Pip's sister, Merrie, just turned four," I said.

"She came to tea," Madam said. "She told everyone she's five."

"I told her what I tell Madam: you're only as old as you feel," Pop said. "Apparently Merrie feels five."

"What are you going to do with your sneakers?" I asked.

"I could keep them in case of an emergency of some sort," Pop said. "But I think I'll be better off throwing them away."

"May I keep them?" I asked.

"You may," Pop said.

"I'm going to nail them to my memory wall that's over my bed," I said.

"I believe you already have a shoe on that wall," Pop said.

"He does," my mom told him. She looked tired.

34

BOB SAVES THE DAY

Pip was in her yard when Sam and I wandered over. Merrie was sitting on the grass painting Pip's toenails.

"Do you want nail polishing?" Merrie asked.

"She's more of a toe painter than a toenail painter," Pip said.

Purple and bright pink polish covered Pip's toe knuckles.

"No thank you," Sam said. "But what color is that?"

"Pinkenpurple," Merrie said.

"Merrie won't pick a favorite color," Pip told us.

"They both are my favorite," Merrie said. "All the other ones are not my favorite."

Anybody could guess that, because pinkenpurple is the only color Merrie wears. Including her shoes.

"My friends are in my house," Merrie said.

"She means Lucy Rose and Jonique," Pip said. "Merrie thinks everybody who comes over is here to visit her."

Merrie gave her a fed-up look. "My friends, Pip-Pip."

"The We-Fix-It Company has been closed," I said.

"By Mrs. Melon," Sam added.

"We need a new way to pay for the teapot," Sam said.

"Come up with a new idea," Pip said.

"Like what?" I asked.

"You'll think of something," Pip said.

Lucy Rose and Jonique came out carrying four glasses.

"Hello, Melonhead," Jonique said. "Hey, Sam. You two can share my lemonade. I'll share with Lucy Rose."

Jonique is generous.

"Was Baltimore fabulinity?" Lucy Rose asked.

"Fabulinity times infinity," I said. "But you won't believe how expensive it is to fix one little dent."

"How much?" she asked,

When Sam told her, Lucy Rose said, "You're going to be twenty-nine before you earn that much money."

Sam was explaining the samovar when an unbeatable idea swooped into my brain.

"Pip!" I said. "Can Sam and I have your carry-out cups from Jimmy T's trash?"

"I guess. They're not as useful as I thought," she said. "They're still in my backsack."

I explained my foolproof money plan.

"We should charge five dollars for five carry-out cups," Sam said.

"Let's get to it," Lucy Rose said.

"What do you need?" Pip asked.

"It's a long list," I told her.

"We have sauce for sure, and gallons of vinegar," Sam said. "My dad and I pour it on sidewalk weeds. It kills them dead."

"Merrie," Pip said. "Can you show Lucy Rose where Mommy keeps our baby cups? But don't drop them or we'll be paying for dents forever."

"Okay, Pip-Pip."

"We need an unbreakable bowl," I said.

"My pink and purple bowl can't break because it's from Nana," Merrie said.

"It can't break because it's plastic," Pip said. "Can we borrow it?"

Merrie took Lucy Rose's hand. "My friend is coming inside my house. You stay on the step."

"Lucy Rose, the peanut butter is in the bottom of the cabinet with the sliding shelf," Pip said.

"What else do we need?" Jonique asked.

"Baking soda," I said.

"We have big sacks of it at Baking Divas," Jonique said.

"Don't forget we need a load of salt," Sam said.

"Can you also bring small bags?" I asked.

"If we can spare any," she said. "We had to order extra because of the Blue Plate Specials."

"Back before you know it," I said, like I was my dad going on a work trip.

When I got back from my house the steps were covered with supplies. Everybody was lying on their stomachs in the grass.

"I'm the sign director and inspector," Sam said. "Pip's sister Maude gave us her used History Fair board."

"I'm drawing the pictures," Pip said.

"I'm stenciling the letter outlines," Lucy Rose said. "You can color them red, Melonhead."

"Merrie's making a different sign because she wants to do it herself," Jonique said.

Merrie's sign had many Ms and Es with extra sideways lines. The rest was fake cursive.

Jonique and I put the supplies in the yard.

"Everybody make an assembly circle," I said.

"I get to wear Mommy's sunglasses for googles," Merrie said.

"Goggles," Pip told her.

"You look like a scientist, Merrie," Sam told her.

"I am a lady with goggles," Merrie said.

"Who wants to fold tinfoil?" I asked.

"I'll do it," Lucy Rose said. "I have experience making mini-napkins at Baking Divas."

Everybody else mixed and filled. I labeled and snapped on the lids. Sam and Merrie put the finished cups in the white bags.

"Can you believe six people put together a business in one hour and sixteen minutes?" I yelled.

"Footpool power!" Sam yelled.

"Grantastic!" Merrie said.

"Let's go sell We-Fix-It kits!" I yelled.

35
WE-FIX-IT KITS FOR SALE

Merrie rode in Pip's lap so the We-Fix-It kits could ride in Merrie's wagon.

"First stop: Madam and Pop's," Sam said.

Pop was watering the lawn when we got there.

"We need help," Lucy Rose told him. "Because none of us are allowed to touch boiling water."

"No one should touch boiling water," Pop said. "It burns."

"She means we can't boil it," Jonique said.

"We couldn't do it at my house because my mom's at acupuncture," Pip said. "Maude is babysitting and Millicent has her geometry tutor."

Madam gave us raspberries and pretzels while the teakettle cooked.

"Where are you setting up your store?" Pop asked.

"By my school," Merrie said.

"In Stanton Park," I said. "A load of people cut through on the way to Union Station."

"Madam," Pop said. "May I take you to the grand opening?"

"Gumbo too," Merrie said. "Gumbo is my friend."

"Before we leave," Pip said, "Sam, spit out your gum."

"I just restarted my record-breaking," he said.

Pip held out her hand. "Spit," she ordered. Then she said, "Show me the top of your melon head, Melonhead."

Pip smashed Sam's gum in my hair.

"Pip-Pip!" Merrie said. "That's bad to do. Mom says."

"You're right, Merrie," Pip said. "Gum doesn't go in hair."

"I'll get it out," Merrie said.

"Yow!" I screamed.

"Quiet," Merrie said. "I am pulling."

* * *

We put our sign up in front of the statue of General Stanton and his horse:

ALL YOUR MISERABLE PROBLEMS SOLVED FOR $5!

BUY A WE-FIX-IT KIT!

FOR PEOPLE OF ALL AGES! MAKES A GREAT GIFT!

"My job is attracting people with my tap dancing," Lucy Rose told her grandparents.

"I told you putting taps on our granddaughter's cowgirl boots was a good investment," Pop said.

"I shouldn't have doubted you," Madam told him.

"Her free-form style is going to catch on," Pop said.

"Does *free-form* mean 'loud and fast'?" I asked.

"In Lucy Rose's case it does," Pop said.

"Madam and Pop," Jonique said, "at Baking Divas, once a few customers come, they all come. So act like you don't know us."

"You can act like you know each other," I told them.

Lucy Rose's boot clattering worked.

Two ladies stopped.

"Welcome, ladies and gentlemen!" I shouted. "Do you have problems that our We-Fix-It kits can help you with? Step right up to the Demonstration Station."

Sam walked up to Madam and screamed, "Is your silver dirty?"

"I'm afraid so," Madam said.

"Is your copper brown?" I asked Pop.

"As brown as acorns," he said. "How did you know?"

I pointed at one of the ladies. "Are your fingers glued together?"

"No," the lady said.

I pointed at the other lady. "Does your dog have gum in its hair? Because the We-Fix-It kit will solve five problems for five dollars!"

A man in a Red Sox baseball cap stopped.

"That's quite a bargain," he said. "Does it work?"

"Everyone, look at this boy's head." Pip waved her arm toward me.

"See the gum!" Jonique said.

I bent over so they could get close looks.

"It's no trick," Pip said. "It's real gum and real hair. Pull it if you want."

Merrie did.

"Now for a dab of Gum-B-Gon!" Sam shouted.

He opened the cup and rubbed a thumb full of peanut butter on the gum spot. "Massage it in. Enjoy the smell. Wipe it off."

We forgot a towel. Sam used his shirt. Actually my shirt that he borrowed.

"Ta-da! The gum is gone!" Sam shouted.

"Would you like to rub his head?" Jonique asked the other lady.

"That's okay," she said.

Another lady walked up pushing a stroller. "Mrs. Deutsch!" Lucy Rose said. "Would you like to put gum in your grandson's hair?"

"Julius's parents are particular," Mrs. Deutsch said. "They think he's too young for chewing gum."

"Even in his hair?" I asked.

"I'm afraid so," she said.

Our teenage friend Justin stopped.

"I need a volunteer," I said. "Who would like to get their fingers glued together?"

No one raised their hand.

"Don't worry!" I said. "This was personally tested by me!"

"Once they're stuck, we'll take them apart," Lucy Rose said. "No pain. Just a relaxing hand rub!"

"You would think after the miracle gum removal you would trust the We-Fix-It kit," I told the crowd.

"I'll volunteer," Justin said.

Jonique squirted two dots of glue on the side of his pointer finger.

"More," Sam said.

"Don't overdo it," Justin said.

Sam held Justin's fingers together.

"This better work," Justin said.

"Now I'm rubbing this boy's glued fingers with We-Fix-It's Glue-B-Gon," Jonique said.

"It glides on," Lucy Rose said.

"It doesn't hurt," Jonique said.

There was quite a lot of clapping over the de-gluing.

A man with a briefcase stopped to watch.

"Do we have a volunteer to test the next formula?" I asked.

"If it doesn't involve my hair, fingers, or any other body part," Mrs. Prosky said.

"This is your lucky day," I told her. "Just dip

Kleenex in this mini-vat of clear gel. Now wipe it across this dirty silver baby cup."

"It's my dirty cup," Merrie said.

"It wiped off the tarnish!" Mrs. Prosky said. "What's in it?"

"Purell," I said.

"Purell-egant," Pip said. "We-Fix-It's Pure Elegant is a top-secret formula that cannot be revealed."

She is the fastest thinker on Capitol Hill.

Mr. Neenobber raised his hand. He was wearing my dad's yellow tie.

"That cup wasn't that dirty," he said. "My high school fencing trophy is so tarnished it's almost black. Will We-Fix-It's Pure Elegant clean it?"

"It will not!" Sam shouted. "But We-Fix-It's Xtra Strong for Xtra Filthy Silver will clean it before your eyes."

"Impossible," Mr. Neenobber said.

Pip held up a silver baby cup. "My sister Maude is the oldest, so her cup is the dirtiest."

"Watch as our assistant Lucy Rose completely covers the inside of this bowl with tinfoil," I said.

Sam waved his arm like he was a magician. "Now

Pip is putting the cup in the bowl, on top of the foil," he said.

Pip tipped the bowl so everybody could see it wasn't a trick.

"Jonique, please pour We-Fix-It's Xtra Strong powder into the bowl," I said.

"Who would like to pour the last ingredient into the bowl?" Sam asked.

"Is it a chemical?" Mrs. Prosky asked.

"It's nothing but H_2O," I said. "Very hot H_2O."

"We can't touch," Merrie said. "'Cause we're kids. Right, Pip-Pip?"

"I am an adult and I'm happy to pour," Mr. Neenobber said. "But you will be disappointed. Water will not clean silver. I've tried."

When the hot water hit the bowl the powder foamed.

"It smells like rotten eggs," Mrs. Deutsch said.

"That's a bonus," I said. "All the smell without the eggs."

I used my slingshot stick to fish out the cup.

"Howza! That's shiny!" Mr. Neenobber said. "My trophy is very large. I'd better buy two kits."

And just like that, he gave Pip a ten-dollar bill.

"I'm not surprised the We-Fix-It kit works so well," a lady said. "The We-Fix-It Company is well-known in our area."

"Are you kids related to the We-Fix-It Company?" Mrs. Deutsch asked.

Jonique pointed to Sam and me. "They are."

"That's all I need to know," Pop said. "I'm buying We-Fix-It kits for all of my adult children. My son in Massachusetts has two sons. And you know how much trouble two boys can get into."

He looked at Sam and me when he said that.

"I have three sons," Mrs. Prosky said. "They all need kits. And I'll take one for myself. My grand-daughter, Violet, is coming for a visit. It'll be wise to have some superglue dissolver on hand."

"Julius is too small for superglue and gum," Mrs. Deutsch said. "But he is at the right age for baby cups."

She bought an upstairs kit and a downstairs kit.

"We saved the best for last," Sam said. "It's called Destructionator!"

"Who has dirty pennies?" I asked.

"I have a change purse full," a lady with yellow hair said.

"Drop them in the Destructionator, please," Lucy Rose said.

"It looks like V8 juice," the lady said.

"V8?" Pip laughed. "Destructionator is a four-part secret formula."

"Four parts," Merrie said, holding up three fingers.

"Make sure I get my money back," the lady said.

I swirled the cup, waited, and fished out the coins.

A man in the back of the crowd said, "That might clean my mother's copper pitcher."

"A pitcher is nothing for Destructionator," I said. "It can clean a chili pot."

The man came to the front.

"It's Mr. Pitt," Sam hissed.

"Live and in person," Mr. Pitt said.

He gave me five bucks. "The glue remover will be useful if I ever get a shoe stuck to my hand," he said.

"As if that could happen," the penny lady said.

The next thing you know, we had a buying stampede.

36

HOW IT FEELS TO BE RICH

Madam and Pop and Gumbo walked with all of us back to Pip's.

"We sold so much there's room in the wagon for Merrie," I said.

"Go fast," Merrie said.

The instant we got to Pip's, Lucy Rose said, "I'm one split of a second away from bursting into smithereens. For heavens to Pete's sake, Melonhead and Sam, count the money!"

"Pile it on the ground!" Pip said.

Sam and I sat on the walkway like frogs.

"Here's Mr. Neenobber's money," Jonique said.

"Here's fifteen dollars," Lucy Rose said.

Pip handed over a big pile. "The guy in the plaid shorts paid in one-dollar bills."

"Put the fives in one stack," Jonique said. "And the tens in another."

"Merrie, that's Melonhead's dollar," Pip said.

Merrie balled it up and made a fist around it. "The lady gave me it, Pip-Pip."

"It's Melonhead and Sam's money," Pip said.

"Merrie's right, Pip," I said. "The lady gave it to Merrie for being a Fix-It girl."

"See, Pip-Pip? I own my money."

"Count it, Melonhead!" Lucy Rose screeched.

Sam took out seven dollars. "Here's your refund, Pop," he said. "Next time pay us after we finish."

"That's good business," Pop said.

When we finished counting I had to do my handwalk of victory and hoot at the top of my lungs.

"I didn't think I'd be near this much money until I'm a pitcher for the Nationals," Sam said.

We took turns holding it.

"Go give it to your mom, Melon-head," Jonique said.

"She'll be proud of all of you," Madam said.

"Thank you, footpool friends," I said. "That was a lot of work."

"If we ever threw pizza sauce and caused our mothers to slip and dent their number-one belonging, you'd help us," Pip said.

"You would never do that," I told them.

"We certainly would not," Lucy Rose said. "Due to our common sense."

We left the girls at Madam and Pop's and skateboarded to my house.

The door was locked, which caused us to ring the bell nonstop. My mom answered the door and the phone at the same time.

"Hello, Traci," she said to the phone. "Hello, boys," she said to us.

I pulled two giant wads of money out of my pocket.

"Whose money is that?" my mom asked.

"Yours," Sam said.

"Not your money, Traci," my mom said. "Adam and Sam have come home with scads of money."

"Earned money," I said. "May I talk to Aunt Traci?"

My mom turned over the phone. "How did children earn so much money?" she asked Sam.

"Hi, Aunt Traci," I said.

"How's Operation Zero?" she asked.

"It turns out Sam and I can't be transformed," I told her. "Even when the reward is something we really, really want."

"Remember, I don't count freak accidents," Aunt Traci said. "Or snafus. Those could happen to anyone."

"It wasn't a snafu," I said. "It was more of an incident."

"I'll be the judge of that," she said.

My mom was fanning herself with bills.

"Oh, my stars," she said. "I counted! This is a lot of money."

"Hold on, Aunt Traci. Mom wants me."

My mother put one hand under my chin and one under Sam's. She tipped our heads up so we were staring in her eyes. "I'm scared to ask. How did you two earn all this money? Did it involve landscaping? Or shoe repair?"

"Nope," I said.

Aunt Traci yelled into the phone, "What are you saying about landscaping?"

She has the supersonic hearing of a bat.

"Adam, can you hear me?" Aunt Traci yelled into her end of the phone.

"It's like you're right here with us," I said.

"Whatever happened I'm sure it wasn't an incident," she said. "So tell me."

"It has to do with Aunt Sylvia's teapot," I said.

She gasped. "Did something happen to the teapot? Because that would be an incident."

"We dented it," I told her.

Aunt Traci gasped.

My mom turned speaker on.

"But the book says if the reward is right, you'll be transformed," Aunt Traci said.

"Traci," my mom said. "We can all hear you."

"Betty!" Aunt Traci said. "It was supposed to be a surprise. Obviously the Follies was the wrong reward."

"It was a great reward," I said. "And we wanted to win it."

"Do you mean bribe?" my mom asked.

"Aunt Traci, this is Sam. We're getting the dent fixed."

"No, we're not," my mom said. "I changed my mind. I want to keep the dent."

"What?" Sam said.

"We made the We-Fix-It kits so you could fix it," I said.

"Don't fix it with a kit," Aunt Traci said. "It's a family heirloom. You need a professional."

"The We-Fix-It kits earned the money to pay Mr. Phillips," Sam said.

"He is very professional," I said.

"I'm not following this conversation," Aunt Traci said.

"I'm confused about the kits and how the boys made so much money," my mom said. "But I'm clear about the teapot. I realized that just like the worn spots and the bent leg, the dent is part of our family history. When my Darling Boy is grown up, I will look at the teapot and think my son and his best friend made that dent while they were trying to invent Destroyernator."

I didn't correct her about the name.

"And when he's grown up he can tell his kids about Sylvia and Irena and how the teapot got that dent," my mom said.

"You know what this means, Mrs. Melon?" Sam said.

"Hello, Jet Ski!" I yelled.

"You're getting a Jet Ski?" Aunt Traci said.

"There's nothing in the world I want less than a Jet Ski," my mom said.

I will never understand the ways of ladies.

37

MORE THAN SATISFIED

We left my mom and Aunt Traci on the phone and checked our messages.

"Open it," Sam said.

Dear We-Fix-It Company,

I've been telling my husband about my dream birdhouse ever since we got married. Now I have it. The birdhouse you made for my birthday has every feature I wanted. It is round and rustic. It blends in with nature and it's waterproof. It is just the kind of house a bird would want to live in. We tucked it into our pear tree. A robin moved in an hour later. I

am recommending We-Fix-It to all the
members of my birding group.

Thank you,
Dr. Ellie West

"A satisfied customer!"
Sam said.

"High twenty-
five," I said.

"Let's recount our money,"
Sam said.

We took it to the dining room so we could see
if, spread out, we had enough to cover the entire
table. My mom was off speaker so we could only
hear what she was telling Aunt Traci. Mostly it was
about how it wasn't sisterly to try to bribe me without permission. I think Aunt Traci was saying she
was sorry.

"It's lucky Pip gave us her carry-out cups," I said.

"Everybody helped out," Sam said. "Even Merrie."

"This is enough money to buy a lifetime supply of
Twizzlers," I said.

"That depends how long you live," Sam said.

"Lucy Rose did a great job getting customers," I said.

We rearranged the money by amount. The highest stack was ones. The lowest stack was tens.

"Maybe this will help our parents consider giving us an allowance," I said.

"Well, even if they make us wait until next year," Sam said, "we know we can figure out money stuff."

"Hot diggity frog!" I yelled. "We have more twenties than tens."

"And almost as many fives as twenties," Sam said.

I turned all the bills president-side-up. "This proves that we can handle money," I told Sam. "And you know what that proves?"

"What?" Sam asked.

"That we're ready to get an allowance," I said.

"I've been ready, Eddie," Sam said.

"People will be amazed that two boys earned so much money," I said.

"With a little help," Sam said. "We wouldn't have been able to do it if Jonique hadn't gotten the baking soda."

"True, but we're the ones who had the experiences that led to the kits," I said.

"We're the inventors," Sam said. "If it wasn't for us going to Baltimore, we wouldn't have learned the silver formulas."

"We're lucky to have friends with Character, Loyalty, and Courage," I told him. "That is actually more valuable than a fleet of dolphins."

"Is your mom still on the phone with Aunt Traci?" Sam asked.

Due to our supersonic brain-to-brain messaging system, I knew what he was thinking.

We burst through the swinging door.

"How can two boys sound like a thundering herd?" my mom asked my aunt.

A herd of what, I don't know.

"Don't hang up!" I said. "We have to ask Aunt Traci a question."

Before she handed over the phone my mom told Aunt Traci, "So we're agreed, you will not offer the boys any more bribes."

Excitement made me scream in

Aunt Traci's ear. "How many half-off Follies coupons do you have?"

"Six," she said.

"She has six!" I shouted.

Sam did a half cartwheel. It would have been whole but my mom said NOT in the house.

"Can we have the coupons?" I asked her.

"Check with your mom," Aunt Traci said. "I promised I'd ask permission before I bribe you."

I pushed the speaker button so I wouldn't have to repeat everything for Aunt Traci.

"Mom," I said. "I know it's rude to talk about money—"

She interrupted. "Is this another plea for allowance?"

"It's about the money we already own," Sam said.

"If we use our Fix-It earnings plus Aunt Traci's coupons, we have enough to take the whole footpool to Follies Park plus half an adult," I said.

"Everybody helped earn the money," Sam said.

"So everybody should get to go," I said.

"Except Merrie because she's too short to go on the fun rides," Sam said.

"She did get to keep a dollar," I said.

"You are a generous friend," my mom said in her I'm About to Say No voice.

"Picture yourself on the Space Race, Mrs. Melon," Sam said.

"Super speed, plus eleven corkscrew spins so you're upside down, and when it can't go faster it drops over a ledge," I told her. "That's two hundred feet in about three seconds."

"The footpool will be berserk with happiness," Sam said.

"Oh, my sweet potato, that will be fun," I said.

"You know I don't enjoy saying no, but I have to think about it," my mom said. "If—"

I didn't let her finish. "Mom, think of the Centrifuge. It spins so fast that your body sticks to the wall, and then guess what? The floor disappears."

Forehead wrinkling is never a good sign.

"Nobody has ever fallen out the bottom," I said. "That I know of."

"Me either," Sam said. "But we ought to let them try. Our footpool friends deserve to take the chance."

My mom took a deep breath.

"Okay," she said. "Let's do it!"

I could not have been more surprised if Mr. Pitt had thrown a shoe at me.

"As long as Aunt Traci goes with us," my mom added.

"What?" Aunt Traci yelled through the phone.

"It would be irresponsible to let the kids go on the rides by themselves," my mom said.

"You go with them," Aunt Traci said.

"I'll be busy taking pictures," my mom said.

"Could I be bitten by a thousand vampire mosquitoes instead of going on the rides?" Aunt Traci asked.

"No," my mom said.

"Don't you worry, Aunt Traci," I said. "We'll be with you."

"We'll start out E-Z P-Z with the Pirate Ship," Sam said. "All it does is flip over."

"You have to come," I told her. "It's the teapot tradition."

"What are you talking about?" Aunt Traci asked.

"Sisters helping sisters," I said. "It's what we do in this family."

"That is a good reason," Aunt Traci said.

"If we take your minivan, we can all go in one car," my mom said.

"Is there room for my dad?" Sam asked. "I'll feel bad if we left him at home."

38

THE DAY OF DAYS

It was dark when we left Follies.

"You know how sometimes you think something's going to be the most glorious, exciting, grandest day on earth? Only it turns out to be just so-so?" Lucy Rose said.

The whole car was silent.

"Well," she said, "this was not one of those days."

"Today was aces!" Sam yelled.

"With syrup on top," Jonique said.

"Fabulinity," Lucy Rose said.

"Times infinity," I said.

"It was even better than the com- mercials," Pip's sister said. "Thanks for picking me, Pip."

"You're welcome, Millicent," Pip said.

The Follies has a load of rules. One is that people who use a wheelchair have to bring a designated rider to go on the rides with them. Pip only needed help getting into the Belly of the Snake flume.

I was sitting in the back row of the minivan between Mr. Alswang and Sam, getting smothered by the stuffed bear in my lap. It's so big you'd think it's real. Except you wouldn't because it's pinkenpurple.

"Can you believe I threw that ball through the Grand Prize hole?" I said.

"I can," Mr. Alswang said.

"The guy who took our tickets said he has only seen one person do it before Melonhead, and that was last year," Lucy Rose told my mom.

"It's hard because the hole is the exact same size as the ball. If you are a fraction of a millimeter off, it hits the wood and bounces off," Sam said.

"I never knew anybody who won a grand prize," Jonique said. "Until now."

I feel really proud of winning that bear.

"I'm proud of riding the Speed Chute thirteen times in a row," Sam said.

"Ditto," I told him.

"The animatronics moved like real Martians," Jonique said.

"That's because they were real Martians," Mr. Alswang said. Then he made that woo-woooo noise that sounds like it's coming from the future.

"I will never go on the teacup ride again," my mom said.

"I will," Aunt Traci said. "But I will not eat pizza before. Or probably after."

It was 11:27 p.m. when we dropped Lucy Rose and Jonique at Madam and Pop's house. They were staying there because Lucy Rose's mom was working late and Jonique's mom has to get to work at four in the morning.

Mr. Alswang said he was so tired Sam would have to carry him into their house. But when Sam tried to pick him up his dad took it back.

At Pip's house I got her chair out. Millicent and

Pip have a system for getting Pip out of cars. It's basically a piggy-back ride. They were up the ramp and unlocking the door when I had a gigantic BOB.

"Mom, take my picture with my bear," I said. "Please."

"Tomorrow," my mom said. "Tonight I'm worn out."

I crawled over the middle row of seats, leaned over to the far back, and pulled the bear over the seats. "Aunt Traci, will you take my picture? I want to remember how great winning feels."

"I think you'll feel that way every time you see the bear," she said.

I stood on the sidewalk and made it look like the bear was riding on my shoulders.

"Got it," Aunt Traci said.

Then I held it in my arms like a giant baby and she took another one.

Then my mom got out and took a picture of Aunt Traci and me and the bear.

"I just realized that I'm the person who got the Follies reward," Aunt Traci said.

"You can bribe yourself all you want," my mom said. "Let's get back in the car."

"I need one thing," I said.

My mom's look was impatient.

I grabbed the stuffed animal and shoved my hands in its mouth.

"Do I look like I'm being attacked by a bear?" I yelled. I ran up the ramp.

"Adam," my mom said. "I've had enough fooling around."

"Coming!" I said. "I just have to get a pencil and paper out of the glove compartment."

I leaned the bear against the front door and put the note in his paws.

Dear Merrie,

Thank you for helping with the We-Fix-It Kits. We missed you at the Follies. You wouldn't have liked it. They have rules against short people. But you will like this rare bear. You can't buy it in a store. The only way to get one is to win it.

From your friend,
Melonhead

P.S. He's named Pinkenpurple, but you can change it if you want.

I got back in the minivan.

"I wish Daddy were with us," my mom said. "He'll be so proud of your generosity."

"I could be proud of your generosity too," I told her. "All it would take is an allowance."

FIVE FIX-IT FORMULAS

CLEANER FOR GOLDEN SILVER
When silver is just a little dirty it looks golden.
Dip a cotton ball into unscented hand sanitizer. Wipe the silver clean. E-Z P-Z.

CLEANER FOR GRAY OR BLACK SILVER
To clean really dirty silver, have an adult boil two kettles of water while you put the plug in the kitchen sink. Next, line the sink with aluminum foil. Line up the silver items on top of the foil, making sure the pieces are not touching. Pour one cup of baking soda and one half cup of table salt on top of the silver. Add extremely hot tap water to the sink until the silver is just covered. You'll need your adult to add one kettle of boiling water. If the tap water was only moderately hot, add the second kettle quickly. The liquid will foam and (bonus!) smell bad. The tarnish will disappear within three minutes. Remove the silver from the sink with tongs and rinse it. To clean another batch, empty the sink, reline with new foil, and repeat directions.

SUPER-GLUE DETACHER
Whenever you're super-glued to something, including yourself, break the bond with patience and petroleum jelly, such as Vaseline, or any lip balm or ointment made with petroleum jelly. Rub gently and slowly. The more glue there is, the more time this will take. Never try to pull your skin apart.

GUM-B-GONE
As you may know from experience, if you fall asleep with gum in your mouth, you will almost certainly wake up with gum in your hair. Solution: Rub a spoonful of peanut butter into the gum. The gum will lose its stickiness and begin to dissolve. What's left will wash out with shampoo.

DESTRUCTIONATOR
To make copper bright, mix together two cups of thick tomato sauce or ketchup, half a cup of white vinegar, and a tablespoon of hot sauce, such as Tabasco. Use a paintbrush to apply to any dirty copper object. Leave on for about five minutes. Then rinse and buff the copper.

ABOUT THE AUTHOR

Katy Kelly has done loads of fix-it jobs. Many of them involved a snafu, a situation, or an incident. Sometimes all three. Eventually she learned to paint a wall, refinish a chair, and operate an electric drill. But when the roof leaks, she calls a professional. This is Katy's ninth book for young readers and the fifth in the Melonhead series. She lives in Washington, D.C.

ABOUT THE ILLUSTRATOR

Gillian Johnson has never invented a cleaning product or built a birdhouse, but she does plan to try some of Melonhead and Sam's fix-it tricks! Gillian is the illustrator of all the Melonhead books. She lives in Oxford, England.